CRY,
THE BELOVED
COUNTRY

A Novel of South Africa

TWAYNE'S MASTERWORK STUDIES

Robert Lecker, General Editor

CRY, THE BELOVED COUNTRY

A Novel of South Africa

Edward Callan

Twayne Publishers • *Boston*
A *Division of* G. K. Hall & *Co.*

Twayne's Masterwork Studies No. 69

Copyright 1991 by G. K. Hall & Co.
All rights reserved.
Published by Twayne Publishers
A division of G. K. Hall & Co.
70 Lincoln Street
Boston, Massachusetts 02111

Copyediting supervised by India Koopman.
Book production by Janet Z. Reynolds.
Typeset by Huron Valley Graphics, Ann Arbor, Michigan.

First published 1991.
10 9 8 7 6 5 4 3 2 1 (hc)
10 9 8 7 6 5 4 3 2 1 (pb)

The paper used in this publication meets the minimum requirements
of American National Standard for Information Sciences—Permanence
of Paper for Printed Library Materials, ANSI Z39.48-1984.⊚™

Printed and bound in the United States of America.

Library of Congress Cataloging-in-Publication Data

Callan, Edward, 1917–
    Cry, the beloved country : a novel of South Africa : [a study] /
by Edward Callan.
        p.   cm. — (Twayne's Masterwork studies ; no. 69)
    Includes bibliographical references and index.
    ISBN 0-8057-8063-7 (alk. paper). — ISBN 0-8057-8109-9 (pbk. :
alk. paper)
    1. Paton, Alan. Cry, the beloved country. 2. South Africa in
literature.   I. Title.   II. Series.
PR9369.3.P37C734   1991
823—dc20   90-48061

Contents

Note on the References
and Acknowledgments

The edition of *Cry, the Beloved Country* used in this study is the most recent New York Collier Books edition: *Cry, the Beloved Country* by Alan Paton, with an introduction by Edward Callan (New York: Collier Books, Macmillan Publishing Company, 1987). This edition is further described on its title and copyright pages as "A Scribner Classic" and "First Scribner Classic/Collier Edition." It includes a foreword by Charles Scribner, Jr., copyright 1986, and a note on the 1987 edition, copyright Alan Paton, 1987. *Cry, the Beloved Country* copyright 1948 and 1976 by Alan Paton. Introduction copyright 1987 by Macmillan Publishing Company, a division of Macmillan, Inc.

Page numbers in this Collier Books edition (included parenthetically in the text) correspond to all other editions published in the United States by Charles Scribner's Sons and Macmillan Publishing Company. Editions of *Cry, the Beloved Country* published in London by Jonathan Cape have different pagination and also a different method of numbering chapters. In New York editions chapters are numbered sequentially throughout; in London editions chapters are numbered within book 1, book 2, and book 3. London editions also carry the subtitle "A Story of Comfort in Desolation."

Acknowledgment is due to the late Alan Paton and also to Anne Paton for permission to quote from works by Alan Paton, including his essays in *The Long View* (1968) and the South African journals, the *Forum, Contrast,* and *Reality.*

Photo by Lensk. Used by permission of Charles Scribner's Sons, an imprint of Macmillan Publishing Company.

Chronology:
Alan Paton's Life and Works

1903	Alan Stewart Paton born 11 January in Pietermaritzburg, Natal, South Africa.
1910	Union of South Africa formed, incorporating two former British colonies, Natal and Cape of Good Hope, and two former Boer republics, Transvaal and Orange Free State.
1915	Enters Maritzburg College, a high school, not a university.
1919	Enters Natal University College (now the University of Natal).
1921	Publishes his first poems, "The Sea" and "Ladysmith (Midnight on the Battlefields)," in *Natal University College Magazine*.
1922	Graduates: B.S. degree, with distinction in physics.
1924	Represents the students of Natal University College at the first Imperial Conference of Students in London.
1925–1928	Teaches mathematics and chemistry at Ixopo High School for white children.
1926	Founds the Students' Christian Association annual boys' camp in Natal with Cyril Armitage and Reg Pearse.
1927	Friendship with Jan H. Hofmeyr begins.
1928	Marries Doris Olive Francis. Joins the staff of Maritzburg College.
1930	David Paton born.
1934	Is seriously ill with enteric fever.
1935	Moves to Johannesburg as principal of Diepkloof Reformatory for African boys.
1936	Joins South African Institute of Race Relations. Jonathan Paton born.
1938	Joins Afrikaner Centenary celebrations of the Great Trek.
1939	Volunteers for military duty in World War II; is found not

	eligible on grounds of essential occupation; becomes chairman of combined YMCA and Toc-H (Talbot House) War Services.
1942	Is appointed to Anglican Diocesan Commission to report on the church and race in South Africa.
1943	Writes series of articles on crime, punishment, and penal reform commissioned by the *Forum*.
1944	Writes and presents address to the National Social Welfare Conference (published as *The Non-European Offender*, 1945).
1946	Takes leave of absence to study penal and correctional institutions in Europe, the United States, and Canada. Begins *Cry, the Beloved Country* in Trondheim, Norway.
1948	In February, publishes *Cry, the Beloved Country* in New York; in May, National party election victory introduces policy of apartheid in South Africa. Resigns from Diepkloof Reformatory. Jan Hofmeyr dies.
1949	Receives Ainsfield-Wolf Award (U.S.) and *London Times* Special Book Award for *Cry, the Beloved Country*. Visits the United States for Broadway opening of *Lost in the Stars*. Begins work on the biography of Jan Hofmeyr.
1951	Publishes *South Africa Today*.
1952	Writes *Too Late the Phalarope* in England.
1953	Joins Liberal party of South Africa as vice president.
1954	Tours the United States to write on race relations for *Collier's*. Receives honorary L.H.D. from Yale. Addresses World Council of Churches meetings, Evanston, Illinois.
1955	Writes *The Land and People of South Africa* for high school students in the United States and Britain.
1956	Is elected chairman of the South African Liberal party, a nonracial party opposed to apartheid. Becomes trustee of the Treason Trial Defence Fund (later called the Defence and Aid Fund) on behalf of Chief Albert Luthuli, Nelson Mandela, and others. Visits New York for dramatized version of *Too Late the Phalarope* by Robert Yale Libott.
1958	Publishes *Hope for South Africa* and *The People Wept*. Becomes national president of the Liberal party. Attends All-African Church Conference in Nigeria. Begins his series "The Long View" in *Contact*. Diepkloof Reformatory closed down. Dr. Hendrik Verwoerd becomes new prime minister of South Africa.
1959	Delivers Stafford Cripps Memorial Sermon in St. Paul's Cathe-

dral, London; sermon published as *The Christian Approach to Racial Problems in the Modern World*. Writes *The Last Journey*, a play about Dr. Livingstone.

1960   State of Emergency declared in South Africa on 30 March. Writes *Mkhumbane* (*Village in the Gulley*), libretto for a musical with music by Todd Matshikiza. Receives the Freedom Award for 1960 from Freedom House, New York. Passport withdrawn on return home.

1961   Publishes *Tales from a Troubled Land* (New York) and *Debbie Go Home* (London). Receives award from Free Academy of Art, Hamburg.

1962   Receives honorary L.H.D. from Kenyon College. Writes play, *Sponono* (with Krishna Shah), produced in Durban and Johannesburg.

1964   Publishes *Hofmeyr* in Cape Town. Broadway production of *Sponono*. Gives evidence for mitigation of sentence at treason trial of Nelson Mandela and others fearing they might receive death sentence.

1965   Publishes *South African Tragedy: The Life and Times of Jan Hofmeyr* (United States edition of *Hofmeyr*); publishes *Sponono* in New York.

1966   Defence and Aid Fund banned. Prime Minister Verwoerd assassinated. Blathazar J. Vorster succeeds him.

1967   In October, Dorrie Paton dies.

1968   Publishes *The Long View*, edited by Edward Callan. Liberal party made illegal under terms of Prohibition of Interference Act. Receives honorary D.L.H. from University of Natal.

1969   Publishes *For You Departed* (*Kontakion for You Departed* in British edition). Becomes founding editor of *Reality: a Journal of Liberal Opinion*. Marries Anne Hopkins.

1970   Passport restored for research on biography of Geoffrey Clayton in England.

1971   Receives honorary L.H.D. from Harvard University, honorary D.D. from Edinburgh University, and honorary L.H.D. from Trent University, Ontario.

1973   Publishes *Apartheid and the Archbishop: The Life and Times of Geoffrey Clayton, Archbishop of Cape Town*. Becomes a Chubb Fellow, Yale University; receives Pringle Award.

1975   Publishes *Knocking on the Door: Shorter Writings of Alan Paton*, edited by Colin Gardner. Receives honorary L.L.B. from University of the Witwatersrand.

1977   Visiting lecturer at University of Michigan at Flint, Western Michigan University, and Michigan State University. Receives honorary L.H.D. from University of Michigan.

1979   Gives Alfred Hoernlé Memorial Lecture, published as *Towards Racial Justice: Will There Be a Change of Heart?*.

1980   Publishes first volume of biography, *Towards the Mountain* (New York).

1981   Publishes third novel, *Ah, but Your Land Is Beautiful,* planned as first volume of a trilogy.

1982   Undergoes heart surgery; abandons trilogy to work on second volume of autobiography.

1983   Celebrates eightieth birthday; tours western United States including Yellowstone National Park, the Grand Tetons, and the Rocky Mountains. University of Cape Town presents lecture series: "Alan Paton at Eighty—A Celebration."

1985   Gives Alfred Hoernlé Memorial Lecture, published as *Federation or Desolation.*

1986   Visits United States for last time. Lectures at Harvard University and at La Salle University, Philadelphia.

1987   Adds new author's note to *Cry, The Beloved Country,* Collier Books edition.

1988   Dies at home in Botha's Hill, Natal, near Pietermaritzburg, on 12 April. Second volume of autobiography, *Journey Continued,* published in November.

Historical and
Literary Context

chapter 1

Historical Background

Alan Paton was born on 11 January 1903, in what was then the British colony of Natal on the east coast of southern Africa. This coastal area was named by the Portuguese explorer Vasco da Gama, who had sailed along that coast on Christmas Day in 1497 while seeking a sea route from Europe to India. In 1903 Natal, which had been primarily Zulu territory until the 1890s, was flanked to the west by another British-ruled territory, formerly a Dutch settlement dating back to the 1650s: the Cape of Good Hope. To the northwest, Natal was flanked by the two former "Boer" republics established by migrant farmers from the Cape of Good Hope in the 1830s, the Transvaal and the Orange Free State. But these were now newly administered by the British following their victory in the Anglo-Boer War of 1899–1902. Therefore, at the time of Paton's birth, South Africa—the country referred to in the title of his famous novel, *Cry, the Beloved Country*—did not yet exist as a national or political entity. It was formed in 1910 when the opposing sides in the Boer War—the colonies of Natal and the Cape, on the one hand, and the republics of Transvaal and the Orange Free State, on the other—joined to form the

Union of South Africa. It was about this time, too, that the descendants of the early Boers began to refer to the dialect of Dutch spoken in South Africa as *Afrikaans* and to refer to themselves, the speakers of this dialect, as *Afrikaners*.

The South African union was brought about in 1910 by representatives of the white settler groups of English and Afrikaner origin in the various territories without consultation with the more numerous African populations who were still largely tribal and rural. As the century progressed old relationships changed rapidly. A population shift from rural areas to industrial centers has characterized the twentieth century everywhere: first in Europe and North America and later in Asia, South America, and Africa. This population shift, with its hopes and disappointments, was also felt in South Africa, most particularly in the great mining and industrial center of Johannesburg where *Cry, the Beloved Country* has its setting. The phrase "all roads lead to Johannesburg" that rises as a refrain in the early part of the novel is replaced at a certain point by the despondent cry: "No second Johannesburg is needed upon the earth. One is enough."[1]

In one of its aspects *Cry, the Beloved Country* reflects the troubled relationships between whites and blacks in the context of the pressures of the flow of population to Johannesburg in the mid-1940s immediately after the Second World War. Beyond the personal tribulations and spiritual trial of its main character, the Reverend Stephen Kumalo, an aging black Anglican priest, the novel's range of vision widens to encompass aspects of the nationwide encounter between black aspirations to human dignity and white fears for the loss of power and privilege. Because of their long history of isolation and their struggle to preserve their language and to keep their social mores intact, white South Africans of Afrikaner origin were particularly determined to retain traditional structures of white privilege and exclusiveness.

Cry, the Beloved Country does not explore this theme, but it is central to Paton's second novel, *Too Late the Phalarope*. Nevertheless it may be useful in a survey of the first novel's historical background to recall that Afrikaner Nationalists have ruled South Africa from the inauguration of the Hertzog administration in 1924 until the present era of the 1990s, with the exception of one interval of eight years. This interval, which seemed to give promise that enlightened liberal policies would eventually prevail in South Africa, lasted only from the outbreak of the Second World War in September 1939 until the general election of 1948. *Cry, the Beloved Country,* written in 1946, reflects some of the hope that prevailed during this promising period in South Africa's long history of conflict.

The present Republic of South Africa—a status proclaimed in 1961 when the policies of apartheid were being vigorously pursued—has its distant origins in the Dutch East India Company settlement at the Cape of Good Hope in 1652. The initial purpose of the Dutch East India Company was not to found a colony at the Cape of Good Hope but to establish a station there for the refurbishment of ships on the long voyage between Holland and the islands of the Netherlands East Indies. (These islands, for a time known as Batavia, now comprise the modern state of Indonesia.) In time, former company servants and new immigrants to the Cape of Good Hope set up as independent farmers—hence the name *Boers* (meaning "farmers") given to their descendants. The number of these early settlers was soon to be augmented by Huguenot refugees from France in 1688 and later by some German immigrants. These newcomers adopted the language and customs of the Boers.

Almost a century and a half passed before England, English law, the English language, and English settlers entered on the scene. Britain first occupied the Cape for strategic reasons in 1795 during the Napoleonic Wars, and it then took permanent possession through a treaty with Holland in 1806. In 1820 the first substantial body of British settlers were brought to the eastern part of the Cape Province near the present cities of East London and Port Elizabeth. In 1824 the first whites settled in Natal at a site later to be called Durban after a British governor of that day.

During the 1830s, groups of Boers, angered by British regulations decreeing equality after the abolition of slavery, trekked inland from the Cape beyond the reach of British rule. Blocked to the east by the pastoral Xhosa tribes against whom they had earlier waged a series of frontier wars, these early migrant farmers, called "voortrekkers," moved northward and founded the republics of Orange Free State and Transvaal—the latter consolidated after a victory over Zulu forces at the Battle of the Blood River in 1838.

The Boers who left the Cape in the first half of the nineteenth century had been slave owners for generations. When the British Parliament in London passed its landmark legislation on slavery—the Abolition of the Slave Trade bill in 1832 and the Abolition of Slavery bill in 1834—these laws mandating the freeing of slaves were immediately enforced in the Cape colony. The slave-owning Boer farmers resented the freeing of their slaves by an occupying power. Perhaps with some reason, they also resented the method of compensation, which was by vouchers payable only in London. They had no choice but to discount these at a fraction of face value to local entrepreneurs. But most of all, they resented being placed on an equal footing before the law with their former slaves. Refusing to live on such terms of equality, some trekked inland under leaders like Piet Retief, giving as one of their reasons—in the words of a letter written by Retief's sister, Mrs. Anna Steenkamp—". . . the shameful and unjust proceedings with reference to the freeing of our slaves; and yet it is not so much their freeing that drove us to such lengths, as their being placed on an equal footing with Christians, contrary to the laws of God, and the natural distinctions of race and color, so that it was intolerable for any decent Christian to bow down beneath such a yoke; wherefore we withdrew in order to preserve our doctrines in purity."[2]

Some of these voortrekkers, led by Pieter Maritz, founded a short-lived Boer republic in Natal with its capital at Pietermaritzburg where Paton was born. But in the face of British opposition they moved on from there to the more permanently established and rigidly segregationist republics of the Orange Free State and the Transvaal. The constitution of the Transvaal specifically declared that in matters of race there should be no equality between blacks and whites in either church or state.

When gold was discovered in the Transvaal in 1886, outsiders from Britain and other European nations flocked in, and a new city, called Johannesburg, arose on the goldfields. The new arrivals demanded enfranchisement, but the less numerous Boers, fearing they might be swamped by newcomers, refused. British intervention in this dispute led to the Anglo-Boer War of 1899–1902. This war was fought between British Imperial forces, based in Natal and the Cape Province, and the local armies of the Boer republics. The long and bitter struggle led to deep resentments that have persisted throughout the twentieth century. The professional British regiments finally prevailed over the Boer commandos. A peace treaty was signed at Vereeniging in 1902. Four years later, in 1906, the British restored the right of self-rule to the Boer territories; and in May 1910 (when Alan Paton was seven years old) the Transvaal and the Orange Free State joined their recent adversaries, Natal and the Cape Province, to form a new country: the Union of South Africa.

Understandably, in a country so divided in its origins, sharp political differences persisted—differences, for example, on questions related to the use of English and Afrikaans as official languages and to the establishment of separate schools and universities with instruction through the medium of these languages. Differences were even sharper on the question of South Africa's participation on Britain's side at the outbreak of the world wars of 1914–18 and 1939–45. Such issues tended to dominate the political concerns of the two white settler groups through the first half of the twentieth century. (At the beginning of book 2 of *Cry, the Beloved Country,* the Natal-born farmer, James Jarvis, is turning these old issues over in his mind as he sits on the hilltop watching the local police car approaching his home.)

More importantly, as already noted, the framers of the South African Union failed to agree on a common policy toward the descendants of the conquered African tribes who greatly outnumbered the whites in the territory as a whole. Some of the more liberal-minded wanted to extend to the whole Union of South Africa the voting rights available in the Cape Province to certain blacks and people of mixed race, but the more conservative majority were unwilling to surrender the traditional Transvaal policy of "no equality in church or state." Repressive policies prevailed from the outset, and two pieces of legislation adopted in 1912 and 1913, the "Natives Land Act" and "Native

Labour Regulation Act," prepared the ground both for the overcrowding of the rural black reservations and for the urban strikes and boycotts of 1946 that provide some of the drama in *Cry, the Beloved Country*.

The first several prime ministers of the new Union of South Africa were former leaders of Boer armies: General Louis Botha, General J. B. M. Hertzog, and General J. C. Smuts. General Botha's fundamental policy as prime minister was one of reconciliation between the two white groups of English and Afrikaans speakers. (Arthur Jarvis, a character in the novel, admires Botha for this.) His successor, General Hertzog, wished, however, to restore a sense of national pride in Afrikaners following their defeat, and he opposed siding with Britain in time of war. General Smuts (later to become a field marshal) supported Botha's policies of reconciliation and sought wider horizons than Hertzog's narrow nationalism. He supported the League of Nations after the First World War, and he wrote the Preamble to the United Nations Charter following the second.

Both Smuts and Alan Paton's friend, Jan Hofmeyr, had served in the cabinet of the coalition government led by Hertzog during the depression years of the 1930s. That was when Hofmeyr, holding the portfolios of both Education and the Interior, introduced legislation transferring juvenile reform institutions from the Department of Prisons to the Department of Education. It was in terms of this legislation that Paton, in 1934, was appointed principal of Diepkloof Reformatory, Johannesburg, and given the task of transforming a prisonlike institution for some 400 delinquent black youths into a school. He accomplished this task with remarkable success and soon earned a high reputation as a penal reformer. It was in pursuit of further knowledge of penal reform, and with the aim of advancement in his profession, that he undertook in 1946 a tour of penal institutions in Europe and America, in the course of which he wrote *Cry, the Beloved Country*.

chapter 2

The Importance of the Work

An essential mark of any great work of literature is its universal acceptance; and evidence of universal acceptance is, in part, an enduring interest in the work through the passage of time and, in part, the response the work elicits from readers whose languages and cultures differ from those of the writer. Both of these measures attest to the remarkable esteem in which Alan Paton's novel *Cry, the Beloved Country* continues to be held.

For more than forty years since its publication in New York in February 1948, and in London six months later, Paton's first novel has continued to sell many thousands of copies annually in the combined sales of the original New York and London editions and the translations into more than twenty languages in Europe, Asia, Africa, and South America. But popularity alone is not a measure of greatness in a work of literature. To be called "great" deservingly, a work must bring its readers to a recognition of some profound truth of the human condition of which they were previously, perhaps, only dimly aware.

After many years as a reviewer for the *New York Times* and other publications, the American literary critic Orville Prescott selected four modern novels from among all those that he had reviewed that he felt deserved to be called great. Prescott says in this regard that one mark of a great novel is that it reveals a belief in the essential dignity of man and in a capacity of some men "to rise to the peaks of wisdom, unselfishness, courage and heroism." Then turning from a consideration of John Hersey's 1950 novel, *The Wall,* to an assessment of Paton's *Cry, the Beloved Country,* Prescott continues: "The second modern novel which I dare call great is the first I have ever read about the tragic plight of black-skinned people in a white man's world." And he elaborates: "Without any of the blind rage which has led so many writers on similar themes into bitterness and dogmatism . . . Mr. Paton wrote a beautiful and profoundly moving story . . . steeped in sadness and grief but radiant with hope and compassion."[1]

Prescott bases his estimate of *Cry, the Beloved Country* on what is one of three necessary considerations of its importance: namely, the degree to which, in its characters and situations, it authentically mirrors the social fabric of South Africa at a given historical moment. A second necessary consideration is the degree to which these characters and situations mirror universal aspects of the human condition beyond their own time and place; and a third is the degree to which some aspects of the novel transcend social or political spheres and reveal a profound spiritual experience.

As to the first consideration, many readers—including Aldous Huxley, for example—have concurred with Prescott that the novel taught them a great deal about a distant country of which they had previously known almost nothing at all. And from the far more informed perspective of someone who knows that country well, the distinguished South African novelist Nadine Gordimer says that South African literature in English "made a new beginning with Alan Paton's *Cry, the Beloved Country* which suggested the need of a Christian solution to the political problem of racialism. It was a book of lyrical beauty and power that moved the conscience of the outside world over racialism and, what's more, that of white South Africa as no book had done before." And she adds: "No piece of writing was to have this effect again until the advent of Athol Fugard's plays, *The Blood Knot* and *Boesman and Lena,* in the late 1960s and early seventies."[2]

While the works of younger writers than Paton—Athol Fugard's plays and the novels of J. M. Coetzee, Andre Brink, and of Nadine Gordimer herself—have brought aspects of South African life vividly before the outside world, there can be little doubt that for many years *Cry, the Beloved Country* was widely seen as the world's window on South Africa. That is a point well made by Charles Scribner, Jr., in his foreword to the 1987 Collier Books edition of the novel. Scribner says *Cry, the Beloved Country* is now a classic work that has found its place in school and college curriculums. And he adds: "It has also become a cultural force of great power and influence insofar as it has depicted the human tragedies of apartheid and brought readers all over the world to an understanding of the perversity and evil of that tragically misguided political system" (xiii–xiv).

But *Cry, the Beloved Country* has qualities that may outlast political systems. Although set in South Africa, a number of its themes have permanent and universal interest: division and reconciliation between fathers and sons; crime, punishment, and the law; hope in circumstances of personal desolation; the movement of rural populations to industrial centers; and the plight of squatters and the homeless in cities that are also the focus of power and wealth. It is through these themes that the novel fulfills the second requirement for an important work of fiction: that some characters and situations mirror universal aspects of the human condition.

It is not surprising, therefore, to find Paton's novel as the subject of a number of graduate theses in Asian universities: in the Philippines, for example, and on the Indian subcontinent where it is available in translations in Hindi and Malayalam. Nor is it surprising to find that the novel was admired by the great Indian statesman Pandit Nehru, who met with Paton in New York to talk about the book and also about the condition of Indian immigrants in South Africa. The noted theological scholar and educator Edmund Fuller aptly characterizes Paton's work: "The measure of his books is that while distilling the essence of South Africa, they speak to many aspects of the whole world. He has struck universal notes, and the world outside his own land honors him for his art, his humanity and his integrity."[3]

Finally, regarding the third measure of the novel's significance, there is the often overlooked theme of a personal spiritual quest to which the subtitle of editions published in London points: "A Story of Comfort in Desolation." (New York editions do not carry this subtitle.) The "desolation" here referred to is the state of near-despair to which the central character, a Christian priest, is reduced at the discovery that his son is a thief and murderer. Regarding this subject, the Anglican theologian Horton Davies says the following in *A Mirror for the Ministry in Modern Novels:* "The constructive meaning of suffering with Christ is 'The Comfort in Desolation' which is the subject of the novel." Davies adds at a later point: "It is not the least of Paton's distinctions that he has provided a moving sociological document and at the same time a theological document, a Christian interpretation of racial tensions and of the spirit whereby they can be overcome."[4] Writing in the *Catholic World,* F. Charles Rooney places *Cry, the Beloved Country* on a different plane from the bulk of modern fiction on the basis of its spiritual theme: "For Paton love, supernatural forgiving love, is the imperative of life; without it life is destroyed. It is the vacuum created by fear and hate that is the cause of all conflict in his novels; his insight into this void has set Paton's novels not only beyond but on a different plane from the bulk of modern fiction."[5]

To Rooney's assessment one may add the more trenchant statement of the great Protestant theologian Reinhold Niebuhr, whom Paton had heard speak in London at an international conference of Christians and Jews shortly before he began to write *Cry, the Beloved Country.* In *Towards the Mountain* Paton cites a response of Niebuhr's in May 1948 to a *New York Times Book Review* interviewer in which Niebuhr said: "The novels that aim directly at being Christian novels are pretty terrible, aren't they? Why do they so seldom succeed? I think, though, that Alan Paton in *Cry, the Beloved Country* succeeds. The book has a genuine religious Christian conflict and has a notably tragic element in it. It is about the only recent religious novel that succeeds."[6]

The Importance of the Work

A final measure of the importance of this work is that even though the intervening decades have seen great changes in South Africa, the circumstances of 1946 depicted in this novel have not lost their power to hold the imagination. This may derive from some of the enduring qualities of the work, discussed above; but as I point out in my introduction to the Macmillan Collier Books edition of *Cry, the Beloved Country:* "It may also derive from an effect of history that affords present-day readers a perspective on the novel in some ways comparable to that of audiences in the Greek tragic theatre who know the outcome of the fateful struggle unfolding before them. Such fore-knowledge quickens the emotions of pity and terror that Aristotle thought proper to tragedy. For readers of the novel conversant with South Africa's intractable social problems, what once seemed merely ominous may now appear to foreshadow tragedy."[7] Nevertheless, interviewed by John D. Battersby of the *New York Times* on 2 April 1988, less than two weeks before his death, Paton said that he thought the central theme of *Cry, the Beloved Country* was still alive in South Africa. "I still believe there is hope," Paton said.

chapter 3

Critical Reception

The first readers of *Cry, the Beloved Country*, while it was still a handwritten manuscript and as yet without a title, were Aubrey and Marigold Burns of Fairfax, California, to whom the American editions of the novel are dedicated. The Burnses had met Paton at a reception in the San Francisco offices of the Society of Christians and Jews on 23 December 1946, and they invited him to spend Christmas with them. Since the Burnses were interested in books and literature, and Aubrey wrote poems, their conversation turned to writing. Paton told them of the manuscript he had almost completed and invited them to read it.

When they did, they were overwhelmed. Aubrey told Paton: "This book will go on living long after you are dead." It was clear to Paton, as he records in *Towards the Mountain*, that reading the novel was a deep emotional experience for the Burnses: "Aubrey blew his nose a great deal and Marigold had recourse to her handkerchief." He adds: "No writer in the world could have asked for more from his first two readers."[1] Years later, Aubrey Burns recalled his first impression for A. Scott Berg, biographer of the famous Scribner editor, Max Perkins, who had accepted Paton's book. Burns told Berg that he found the manuscript difficult to read, partly because of the handwriting and partly because of the strange names, "but chiefly because it is difficult to read small script through water—tears rose up as from a mountain spring, from one phrase to another and from one emotion to another."[2] According to Berg, it took Burns only a moment to realize he was reading a work of genius.

When the Burnses pointed out to Paton that the story had, as yet, no title, the three of them agreed to propose titles by secret ballot. Each wrote a title on a piece of paper, and when the papers were compared they discovered that each had written the same phrase drawn from the book, "Cry, the Beloved Country." Like millions of readers worldwide in the years that followed, the Burnses knew almost nothing about South Africa. Yet their reading of the book touched them; and they were so imbued with a sense of its value that they set to work to have it hurriedly typed and submitted to publishing houses. In time, Paton repaid their generosity by having his publisher accord them ten percent of royalties as an agent's fee.

Although the Burnses were lovers of literature, they were not professionals in the field. But the next reader of *Cry, the Beloved Country* was unquestionably a professional. Max Perkins, of Charles Scribner's Sons, was well known in literary circles, and his fame as an editor of genius was widespread. He had worked closely with such writers as F. Scott Fitzgerald, Ernest Hemingway, and Thomas Wolfe. He was a believer in the neoclassical principle that outstanding works of literature both delighted readers through excellence of style and instructed them through new visions of reality. He was certain, said his biographer, that the immortal books addressed themselves to the literate and the masses alike: "The great books," he said, "reach both."[3]

On receiving a copy of a portion of Paton's manuscript from Aubrey Burns, Perkins responded within two days saying he would like to meet the author. Paton, who had a passage already booked on a boat leaving soon from Halifax for Cape Town, could only spend a very short time in New York. He arrived at the offices of Charles Scribner's Sons late on a Friday afternoon, 7 February 1947. When

Perkins, with Paton's manuscript in hand, led him to a man in another office and said, "Charles, we must accept this," Paton did not know that the other man was Charles Scribner. By then it was closing time, and Perkins brought Paton to a bar where, as Paton wrote to Aubrey Burns: "He lifted his glass in toast, but didn't say what the toast was. . . . He said, of course you may not make much money. We can't guarantee that the public will buy." They met again on Monday morning and Paton felt a little more reassured when Perkins said: "You are not to worry because you're not going away with a contract. I don't see how Scribner's could refuse it."[4] Nevertheless, Paton embarked on his return voyage to South Africa still puzzled by Perkins and uncertain whether or not his book was accepted.

Soon after he arrived back in Johannesburg, Paton received Perkins's critique of *Cry, the Beloved Country*. In it Perkins said he felt that the third part of the novel on the conditions in the tribal reserves came as something of an anticlimax after the book reached its dramatic peak in the trial scene. Perkins suggested that some critics might disparage it on those grounds. Paton was prepared to revise the book in response to this opinion, which he felt had merit. But within a month, Perkins sent Paton the contract for *Cry, the Beloved Country* with an accompanying letter in which he said he had come to realize that: "the real protagonist is the beautiful and tragic land of South Africa, but if you come to the human hero, it is the Zulu pastor, and he is grand."[5]

Then, turning to the final third of the book which Paton was prepared to revise because of Perkins's earlier reservations, he said: "One might say that the last third of the book is something of an anticlimax, but I don't think one should look at it in a conventional way. It gives an extraordinary realization of the country and of the race problem, not as a problem but as a situation." To this revised interpretation of book 3, Perkins added of the novel as a whole: "It is a sad book, but that is as it should be. So was the Iliad and so is the Bible." And he concluded: "But as Ecclesiastes says, 'The earth endureth for ever.' "[6] By this last remark Perkins showed that he recognized that one of the great themes of the novel is the indispensability of hope. He said nothing further about revision; and the novel was published as Paton wrote it.

Unheralded prior to its publication on 2 February 1948, *Cry, the Beloved Country* had a small advance sale of about 3,000 copies. Yet before the year was out it was acclaimed by critics and by the reading public alike. Rarely has a first novel by an unknown author achieved such popularity or succeeded in retaining so large a measure of popularity with the passage of time. (When Paton died forty-four years later, on 12 April 1988, it had sold more than 15 million copies in twenty languages.) The early reviewers in the United States were almost unanimous in praising the refreshing simplicity of the novel's language and the deep humanity of its theme. As Charles Scribner, Jr., said in his foreword to the 1987 Collier Books edition: "When the book was published it virtually exploded on the literary scene. Review after review heralded it as a literary classic. . . . The book became an instant bestseller" (xiii).

In the *New York Times,* the noted reviewer Orville Prescott describes *Cry, the Beloved Country* as "a beautiful and profoundly moving story, a story steeped in sadness and grief but radiant with hope and compassion. I believe it is certain to rank as one of the finest novels of the year." And he said further that as "a picture of the fear and suspicion and hatred which haunt all South Africans black and white, it is brilliant."[7] In a later article in the *Yale Review,* Prescott says that Paton's novel is the finest he has ever read about the tragic plight of black-skinned people in a white man's world; and he stresses his perception that *Cry, the Beloved Country* entirely lacks "the bitterness, dogmatism and exaggerated melodrama which disfigure most fictional treatments of race relations." He reiterates and amplifies his earlier assessment of the novel: "It is steeped in sadness and grief over man's inhumanity to man; but it is illuminated by hope and compassion. There is a generosity of spirit here which is as rare as it is beautiful and moving."[8]

In a very perceptive and thoughtful review in the *New York Times Book Review,* Richard Sullivan finds *Cry, the Beloved Country* to be "a beautiful novel, a rich firm and moving piece of prose." Sullivan was one of the first to remark on the profound spiritual drama embodied in the novel and also on the universality of its themes. In his review, he says that its matter and locale may be strange to American readers, "but its writing is so fresh, its understanding so compassionate, that to read the book is to share intimately, even to the point of catharsis, in the grave human experience treated. For what in other hands might have made merely an interesting sociological document is here intensified into an urgent, poetic and profound spiritual drama, universal in its implications."[9]

Almost every aspect of *Cry, the Beloved Country* was singled out for praise by one early reviewer or another: its language and style, its characters, its intellectual honesty and compassion, and its universal scope. On its language and style, Margaret Carson Hubbard in the *New York Herald Tribune Weekly Book Review* remarks that as a novel, a story of lives unfolding, *Cry, the Beloved Country* stands by any standards; but she feels that the quality of the style is, above all, a new experience: "Here, in English, is a new cadence, derived from the native tongues. English words are used with the limpid rhythms of Zulu and Xosa, as picturesque, as simple in expression, yet as delicately suggestive, as those languages."[10] And Richard Sullivan, quoted above on the universality of the novel's themes, has this to say on "the simple splendor of its language" in the same review: "In *Cry, the Beloved Country*, what is presumably a Zulu idiom is rendered into English full of strange new grandeur."[11]

Many other reviewers were struck by the freshness of the novel's style. Noteworthy among these was Lewis Gannet, who was later to write an introduction that graced the Scribner paperback editions until 1987. Reviewing *Cry, the Beloved Country* in the *New York Herald Tribune*, Gannet says: "Beside the sprawling verbosity, the tawdry cleverness of currently touted novels, *Cry, the Beloved Country* shines with a great radiance."[12] Later, in his introduction to the 1959 Scribner paperback edition, Gannet begins by saying that although *Cry, the Beloved Country* did not fit into any pattern of the modern novel, it was likely to be longer remembered than any other novel of 1948: "It stands by itself; it creates rather than follows a tradition. It is at once unashamedly innocent and subtly sophisticated. It is a story; it is a prophecy; it is a psalm. It is passionately African as no book before it had been; it is universal. It has in it elements of autobiography: yet it is selfless." Gannet concludes his introduction by stressing again the uniqueness of the book: "*Cry, the Beloved Country* stands alone. We have had many novels from statesmen and reformers, almost all bad; many novels from poets, almost all thin. In Alan Paton's *Cry, the Beloved Country* the statesman, the poet and the novelist meet in unique harmony."[13]

But the style and language were not the only qualities of Paton's novel to draw unstinted praise. Reviewers also commended the quality of Paton's characterizations. James Stern, writing in the *New Republic,* is one such enthusiast: "I should like to predict that in the Reverend Stephen Kumalo, Paton has created an immortal figure. If there is a man who can read the tragedy of Kumalo's life with eyes dry, I have no desire to meet him."[14] Charles J. Rolo, reviewing the novel in the *Atlantic Monthly,* says: "The mainspring of this unusual book is saintliness. The hero, an old Zulu minister, the Reverend Stephen Kumalo, is a feat of characterization rare in the modern novel: a convincing portrait of a saintly man."[15]

Again, more than one reviewer commented on the novel's compassion and intellectual honesty. In the *Commonweal,* A. W. Foulke says: "The stature of this book comes from the spirit of compassion and intellectual honesty which set it apart from many others dealing with the same theme. It is more than just a fictionalized social tract."[16] And Adrienne Koch's views in the *Saturday Review of Literature* fully concur: "Rarely have professional story tellers in recent years achieved the affecting truthfulness, the shining warmth, and analytic sanity of this book."[17] And in the *San Francisco Chronicle,* Edith James remarks on the novel's universality as well as its compassion, and like many of the other reviewers she recognizes that the book has lasting qualities and will endure: "Here is a book which presents a clear and compassionate picture of one land and yet is universal in its basic theme. It is a book to read and enjoy and then to read again and ponder over."[18]

In the late summer of 1948—some six months after the American first edition—*Cry, the Beloved Country* was published in England by Jonathan Cape with the subtitle, "A Story of Comfort in Desolation." The novel again met with popular and critical approval, and it was accorded a Special Book Award from the London *Times*. But English newspaper reviewers differed from their American counterparts earlier in the year in one respect. They placed greater emphasis on the representation of race relations in South Africa—most probably because, in the meantime, public attention had been focused on the political campaign and election that brought apartheid to South Africa. A short notice in the *Times Literary Supplement,* for example, says that Kumalo's tragic search is "linked with a serious and moving analysis of South Africa's most disturbing problem."[19]

The great success of *Cry, the Beloved Country*—and the National Party's election victory—emboldened Paton to resign his government post at Diepkloof Reformatory and devote himself to writing. He said in a broadcast talk: "I have left the public service, but not with any intention of living in idleness or ease. I want to interpret South Africa honestly and without fear. I cannot think of any more important or exciting task."[20]

Not surprisingly, *Cry, the Beloved Country* had a mixed reception in South Africa, where it did not become generally available—in the London edition from Jonathan Cape—until after the fateful election of May 1948 that brought the Afrikaner nationalists to power. There were, of course, earlier reports of the novel's extraordinary reception in the United States, including an article in an April 1948 issue of the popular South African magazine the *Outspan*. This article reported that the first American printing sold out on the first day, 2 February 1948, and that the book was already in its sixth printing. Many white South African English speakers admired the book, particularly for the beauty of its lyric passages; and it soon became regarded as the most significant novel of South African life since Olive Schreiner's acknowledged masterpiece, *The Story of an African Farm*, published in the 1880s. But some of these English speakers were affronted by its picture of the plight of urban Africans, which they deemed sentimental or propagandistic. An extreme example of this outlook was provided by an angry white farmer in Zululand who wrote to Paton (as he reports in *Journey Continued*) condemning *Cry, the Beloved Country* as "a pack of lies; an act of treachery towards his country; and a lot of sentimental twaddle."[21]

A much higher proportion of Afrikaans speakers disliked the novel—and more intensely—for some of the same reasons. With one exception—*Die Burger*, Cape Town—no Afrikaans-language newspaper reviewed Paton's novel. Had they read it, many Afrikaner nationalists would have disbelieved its picture of South Africa—as did the wife of Prime Minister D. F. Malan, who said to Paton at the South African premiere of the film version of *Cry, the Beloved Country*: "Surely, Mr. Paton, you don't really think things are like that?"[22]

The greater defensiveness of Afrikaners and their more passionately intense response to anything deemed critical of white South Africa is bound up with their historical experience and fervent nationalism: they trekked into the interior in the nineteenth century to preserve their way of life from British influence; they developed a new language of which they are intensely proud; and many among them were determined to redress the humiliation of defeat at the hands of the British in the Boer War. Interviewed for *Time* magazine, Paton sought to account for the less defensive posture of English speakers. He said: "We never trekked, we never developed a new language, we were never defeated in war, we never had to pick ourselves out of the dust." He continued: "Both Afrikaners and English have a love of country, but the Afrikaner's love is in general more fierce, more emotional, more aggressive. It is his history that has done it to him."[23] These remarks, besides helping to explain the coolness of more nationalist-minded Afrikaners to Paton's novel, also throw light on the passage from which the title derives: "Cry, the beloved country, for the unborn child that is the inheritor of our fear. Let him not love the earth too deeply. . . . for fear will rob him of all if he gives too much" (80).

Nationalism of another kind, particularly as it emerged in its more extreme form, also had some bearing on attitudes to *Cry, the*

Beloved Country in South Africa. During the decades of the 1960s and 1970s when the oppression of apartheid was at its harshest in South Africa, and when black nationalist organizations were banned and their leaders imprisoned or exiled, there was a tendency among some black South Africans to view Paton's novel as limited by the white perspectives of its author and therefore less than authentic. Such reactions are not unusual when works of literature are judged from a passionately nationalistic standpoint. Perhaps the classic instance of this in English literature of the twentieth century were the riots in Dublin in 1907 when J. M. Synge's masterpiece, *The Playboy of the Western World,* was first staged at the Abbey Theatre. According to W. B. Yeats, there were 70 policemen in the theater on the final night and some 500 keeping order in the streets outside. And while nationalistic resentment with the theater's other leading playwrights, Lady Augusta Gregory and W. B. Yeats, did not reach the same heights, some Irish nationalists of Gaelic-speaking and Catholic backgrounds found it distressing that members of the Anglo-Irish Protestant ascendancy should seem to speak for Ireland. In like manner some black South African nationalists resent the depiction of black plight by white writers like Paton. But that view, which values literature only to the extent that it appears to support some cause, is far from universal.

One notable account of *Cry, the Beloved Country* from a black South African perspective is that of the poet Dennis Brutus, who, for his active opposition to apartheid, was imprisoned for years on Robben Island where Nelson Mandela and other political leaders were also imprisoned. Presented at a symposium on protest and conflict in African literature, this otherwise thoughtful and balanced account is in some degree limited by the topics Brutus addresses: generally, the literature of protest; and specifically, "Protest against Apartheid."

In Brutus's view, "Paton is interesting because he started what seems to me almost a new era in South African writing. . . . Other people had written not much less competently the sort of thing which Paton wrote in *Cry, the Beloved Country,* but somehow they did not set in motion the kind of cycle which Paton did." And he elaborates: "One must not think in color categories, but it is very difficult to resist thinking of Alan Paton as a white man, a sympathizing white man standing outside the South African society . . . and reducing it to what is almost a parable; . . . but telling a story which moved people and caught people's attention. It became a film, it became a play, and, among other things, it touched certain springs in the feelings of white South Africans." Brutus concludes, adverting to the topic of his address: "This is Paton's protest against apartheid. . . . Whatever he has said elsewhere in terms of the novel, I think he has never matched the simple direct attack which he made in *Cry, the Beloved Country.*"[24] In Brutus's eyes, Paton's later political pamphlets, such as *The People Wept,* constituted a more significant attack on apartheid than the novel did.

Apart from the portion of Brutus's address devoted to *Cry, the Beloved Country,* there are no substantial appraisals of Paton's novel from a black South African standpoint; nor are there any from an Afrikaner nationalist standpoint. To date, the comparatively few substantial published accounts of the novel remain those already mentioned: articles by Orville Prescott, Horton Davies, and Edmund Fuller; my own chapters on the novel in *Alan Paton* (1968; rev. ed. 1982); and studies by Martin Tucker and Sheridan Baker, respectively, that call for comment.

In his detailed study, *Africa in Modern Literature,* Martin Tucker divides South African novelists into two categories. He says one category, in which he includes Olive Schreiner and Doris Lessing, represents "the spirit of apartness," and the other, including Peter Abrahams, Dan Jacobson, and Nadine Gordimer, represents "the spirit of forgiveness." He puts forward *Cry, the Beloved Country* as the most famous and one of the earliest novels of forgiveness, and he elaborates: "The second half of the novel has had a profound influence on the thoughts of non–South African readers, even if its message is currently being derided by some black South African critics. For Paton's novel is the supreme instance of the kind of novel of forgiveness which calls for the construction of love on the ruins of tragedy."[25]

The final study requiring passing comment here is Sheridan Baker's "Paton's Beloved Country and the Morality of Geography" that appeared in the journal *College English* in 1957. Classical works employing allegorized, or "moral," landscapes include Dante's *Divine Comedy* and Bunyan's *Pilgrim's Progress;* and modern works similarly employing landscape with a psychological rather than religious purpose include some of W. H. Auden's poems, one of which is appropriately titled "Paysage Moralisé" (i.e., "Allegorized Landscape"). Yet for all of Baker's tortuous theorizing, Paton's novel cannot be fitted into this category.

Baker's essay might be passed over in silence had it not become widely available in a volume Baker edited in the series of "Scribner Research Anthologies." This book, in addition to providing the text, supplied students with instructions for making note cards and also with a package of essays and commentaries related to the text from which they could compile term papers with appropriate footnote citations. Starting off with the unjustified assumption that Paton "even readjusted South Africa's profile to resemble that moral terrain that both Dante and Bunyan traveled,"[26] Baker embarks on a series of freewheeling associations—including the association of one character, Arthur Jarvis, with God—that are too numerous to be refuted here. The journal, *College English,* printed a response by Harry A. Gailey, an authority on African history. This response, "Sheridan Baker's 'Paton's Beloved Country,' " also fortunately included in the anthology, comments systematically on some of Baker's more wayward statements "that give an erroneous view of Paton's social novel and of South Africa"; and it points out that "the most obvious fault lies in the thesis that Paton consciously uses the geography of South Africa symbolically."[27]

Despite the objections of some South Africans, very largely on political grounds, Paton's first novel was widely read in his home country when it became available there in the latter part of 1948. For a time, according to some reports, it outsold all other books except the Bible. And it was subsequently read not only in English but also in Zulu translation. The majority of his South African readers who were not blinded by prejudice could readily understand why American and British reviewers had greeted *Cry, the Beloved Country* with a chorus of praise.

Critical Reception

Such a reception for a first work by a previously unknown writer is rare; and almost unanimous affirmations of the universality of a new work, and of its lasting qualities, are still rarer. Ordinarily a work dealing with so profound a theme and showing such mastery of style and characterization appears as the fruit of long apprenticeship in the art. Paton's apprenticeship was limited. From his college days onward, he had written poetry, fiction, and drama, but only as an avocation. This early development of his talents as a writer was, no doubt, important when he set out to compose his novel; but even more important was the fact that, at age forty-five, he had lived through experiences to which he had devoted profound thought, such as his service on an Anglican synod and his reformatory work among black South Africans.

A Reading

chapter 4

From a Dark Wood

"In the middle of the journey of our life I found myself in a dark wood where the right way was obscured," wrote Dante at the beginning of his allegorical journey, set in his own thirty-fifth year. Alan Paton was forty-five, and past the middle of his days, when out of his longing to find a path toward freedom from South Africa's moral dilemmas, he began to write in fictional form his vision of how men of good will in that troubled country might find emancipation from inbred racial fears and prejudices.

At least twice in his life before, Paton had found himself in the dark wood of crisis, and each time he had sought a new way out. After a serious illness and six months of convalescence in 1934, at age thirty-one, he decided that teaching in white, upper-class preparatory schools was not the best path toward solving pressing South African problems. At that juncture, he accepted the principalship of a reformatory for black youths in Johannesburg, the great industrial and gold-mining center, and he undertook the task of transforming that virtual prison into a training school. Some seven years later he again discovered himself in the dark wood of dilemma. That was when his work on an

Anglican Church study commission brought him to the stark realization that South African notions of white supremacy could not be reconciled with Christian principles. Then in September 1946, homesick and lonely in Trondheim, Norway, he found a way of objectifying his vision of "what might be" in South Africa in the form of a novel.

To accomplish this he drew much from the two earlier experiences. A significant part of the action of Cry, the Beloved Country is set in and around Diepkloof Reformatory in Johannesburg, and the story involves the fate of a black delinquent youth who had been an inmate there. Another significant part in the novel involves a man committed to the Christian way in its fullest sense: the Reverend Stephen Kumalo, an Anglican priest. Therefore, since the novel is informed by Paton's deepest personal experiences in earlier circumstances that changed his life, a brief account of each may prepare the way for better understanding of the work.

Paton's earlier attempts to find a way out from the constraints of conventional South African racial attitudes involved him in three kinds of action: practical, intellectual, and spiritual. The practical attempt was, of course, his work at Diepkloof Reformatory. When Paton arrived at Diepkloof he found a prison surrounded by a double barbed-wire fence and staffed by armed warders. The more than 400 boys, ranging in age from ten or so to twenty, were locked into rooms at night in groups of twenty supplied only with two buckets—one containing water, and the other for urination and defecation. In the mornings the stench was unspeakable. Paton's first step towards reform was to persuade the reluctant warders to leave the dormitories open at night so that the boys could use the lavatories. One result of this first step in using freedom as his instrument of reform was that "typhoid fever, which had been the scourge of the reformatory and the cause of many deaths, almost completely disappeared."[1]

Paton intentionally chose freedom as his instrument of reform at Diepkloof. To transform that virtual prison into a school he set about organizing it as a place of education and rehabilitation based on "increasing freedom, increasing responsibility, increasing privilege, and increasing temptation."[2] Newly committed boys were housed in a closed dormitory. When they proved themselves trustworthy, they were transferred in small groups to the care of a housefather and housemother and given freedom to roam the large reformatory farm. Later, they were allowed the privilege of weekend visits to their families. In time, the most trustworthy senior boys were permitted to work for employers outside the institution, and to live in hostels where they paid part of their earnings for their keep. They were encouraged to save the rest for the time of their release. Absalom Kumalo in the novel participates in this program, and one of the few things he leaves behind before his death is a savings book.

There were, of course, failures and frustrations at Diepkloof Reformatory. Paton recalls one of the worst of these in his autobiography, *Towards the Mountain,* where he says that by the time he left Diepkloof tens of thousands of boys had been given home leave at weekends, and of these only about a hundred had not returned. One of this hundred did the kind of thing that Paton feared most. On Sunday, when he was due to return, the Diepkloof staff heard on the radio that hundreds of police were searching for a young black man who had killed a white woman in the pantry of her house: "It was supposed she had heard a noise in the pantry and had gone to investigate. Pantries usually have only one door and she was standing in it. The young man . . . struck her down and when found, she was dead."[3] Paton and his Diepkloof staff had a premonition, that Sunday, that the boy who had not returned might well be the murderer. It turned out that he was; and after his trial, he was sentenced to death. It was, no doubt, a recollection of this incident that led to the creation of Absalom Kumalo in *Cry, the Beloved Country* and that brought members of the reformatory staff into the story also.

While still engaged in his work at Diepkloof, Paton branched out on the intellectual path of a writer and lecturer on current affairs. He had a new vision to offer on topics of penal reform, crime, and other social and racial issues. One of the journals he wrote for, which commissioned six articles from him on crime and punishment in 1943, was the *Forum,* based in Johannesburg. Founded in 1938, the *Forum* was a South African journal of opinion that supported Jan Hofmeyr's liberal views. Paton remembered its first appearance as "an exciting event"; and his excitement at its opposition to the proapartheid policies of Dr. D. F. Malan carried over into this description, published some twenty-five years later in his biography of Hofmeyr: "The first appearance of the *Forum* on 4 April 1938 was an exciting event. It was a challenge to the whole Malanite creed with its isolationism and racial exclusiveness. . . . Its pages were large, full of good stuff, and all for sixpence."[4] Editorially, the *Forum* stood for freedom of thought and speech, and "the fearless expression of opinions by others"; and almost half a century before the political crises of the 1990s in South Africa, it also stood for a gradual extension of voting rights to all races.

The *Forum* immediately opened a debate on the question of faith and fear in South Africa that was to become a familiar theme in Paton's later writings, including *Cry, the Beloved Country*. The first issue of the *Forum* declared editorially: "We believe that if the Afrikaner were released from fear for his culture, there would be more chance of a constructive contribution to the Native question." An early issue of the *Forum* published an article by Jan Hofmeyr with the title "Faith and Fear in Politics," in which he defines a "liberal" as someone who "asserts the essential value of human personality as something independent of race or colour." Against this he sets the white South African self-styled "realist" who, faced with the numerical preponderance of the native African population, "resorts to a policy of repression which is based on fear"; but, says Hofmeyr, "he fails to see the further fact that fear engenders hatred."[5]

Readers of *Cry, the Beloved Country* will recognize this argument as a recurring theme in the novel—often on the lips of the black Johannesburg priest, Msimangu: "I have one great fear in my heart that one day when they are turned to loving, they will find we are turned to hating" (40). This theme of going forward in faith, not fear, the keynote of the first *Forum* editorial, is also at the heart of the essay by the murdered man, Arthur Jarvis: "Private Essay on the Evolution of a South African," in book 2 of *Cry, the Beloved Country*.

Even more relevant to the themes of *Cry, the Beloved Country* is Paton's series of six articles on crime and punishment published in the

Forum during 1943–44. One of the main topics of this series, pertinent to a study of *Cry, the Beloved Country,* is the need for the restoration of human dignity. The series proposes that the best way to deter crime is to restore to each person a feeling of social significance: "To mean something in the world is the deepest hunger of the human soul, deeper than any bodily hunger or thirst, and when a man has lost it he is no longer a man." Beyond that, these articles say, the great need is to reform society itself so that every man can take his place in it with dignity. "There is one supreme reason why men do not commit crime and that is because they have goals, interests, ideals, homes, children, savings schemes. The home, the church, the association, have given them worthy aims and have expressed—and continue to express—social approval of their lives and actions. They do not commit crime—not because they are afraid— but because they are socially significant."[6]

The final article in Paton's series on crime and punishment, titled "Who Is Really to Blame for the Crime Wave in South Africa?" appeared in the *Forum* of 15 December 1945, a few months before his departure on 8 June 1946 on the international tour of penal institutions during which he wrote *Cry, the Beloved Country.* This article has a special relevance to *Cry, the Beloved Country* because it shows that the basic themes of the novel were uppermost in Paton's mind before he embodied them in fictional form. Remarkable also for the urgency of its tone, this article begins by warning against the tendency to dismiss outbreaks of crime among Africans as part of a general postwar phenomenon, while ignoring the more important underlying cause.

According to Paton the underlying cause of African crime in Johannesburg was the disintegration of tribal society under the impact of Western economy and culture: "For a long time the full dangers were not seen, but fathers and sons and daughters went to work in Johannesburg and sometimes never came back." In time, Africans tried to set up new homes in cities; but without the powerful support of tribal custom, these new city dwellers "began to experience with bewilderment and shame the shocks of disobedient children, pregnant daughters, delinquent sons." Home life decayed in the overcrowded slums; and it also decayed in the tribal reserves, "where men did not come back, and where women went away to look for them and often found someone else."[7]

Quite obviously, several of the characters in *Cry, the Beloved Country* are embodiments of a number of the general cases presented in this article. Among those, for example, who went away to work was the husband of Gertrude, who, in turn, went to look for him and found others instead. And in Abasolm and his girlfriend we have instances of a delinquent son and a pregnant daughter.

The second part of this *Forum* article on the crime wave in South Africa raises the question, "How is society to be restored?" It responds by saying that moral and spiritual decay can be stopped only by moral and spiritual means. Restoration therefore requires opportunities for work, education, and the growth of self-respect, in order to create a climate where decency and morality can flourish. Paton repeats the theme of his earlier articles in the series: "Men obey the laws when they are pursuing worthy goals, working for some good purpose, making the most of their seventy years, using their gifts."[8]

In *Cry, the Beloved Country* those rural Africans who have come to the city must learn to be part of a new industrial society with its money economy, its factories, transport systems, and housing needs. Stephen Kumalo and those closest to him—his wife, for example, and Msimangu, and Mrs. Lithebe—rely on the precepts of their church for guidance. They place a very high value on education and, not surprisingly, on the practical matter of budgeting their meager resources. The reader is constantly aware of the money they have accumulated in their post office savings books and their careful spending of it. (By contrast those who have gone astray, like Gertrude, are thriftless.) The struggle to live decently in a money economy is exemplified by the woman in Alexandra Township who reluctantly agrees to let someone rent space in her already crowded house as she calculates her needs. And the young social worker from the reform school, whose job it was to prepare delinquents like Absalom for society, has concern for their management of money as well as their need for job skills.

Besides taking a practical approach to social problems at Diepkloof and searching for intellectual answers in his writings, Paton also found himself faced with white South Africa's deepest spiritual dilemma. One of his most significant spiritual experiences resulted from an initiative of the new Anglican Bishop of Johannesburg, Geoffrey Clayton, whose biography Paton later wrote under the title, *Apartheid and the Archbishop.* In 1941 Bishop Clayton named Paton a member of a diocesan commission appointed "to discover what it believed to be 'the mind of Christ for South Africa.' " In 1943 this commission presented its report, *The Church and the Nation,* which examined the problems of black poverty, racial discrimination, and voting rights. There can be little doubt that Paton had a significant part in the writing of this report. Paton felt that his work on this commission was a turning point in his life. He says it convinced him that South African notions of white supremacy could not be reconciled with Christian principles: "As for myself, having lived for thirty-eight years in the dark, the Commission opened for me a door, and I went through into the light and I shut it against myself, and entered a new country whose very joys and adversities were made resplendent by the light."[9]

There remained one deep experience, the following year, that allowed Paton to see his way out of the dark wood even more clearly. (In *Cry, the Beloved Country* the elder Jarvis undergoes a somewhat similar experience at the funeral of his son.) There was a white woman in Johannesburg among those who shared Paton's concern for penal reform, improved race relations, and the principles that the *Forum* stood for. Although in poor health, this woman, Edith Jones, continued to help black women who were her friends to organize troops of girl scouts, called Wayfarers, in remote rural areas. A month after Paton had driven her from Johannesburg to visit one of these remote areas, she died. He found her funeral a deep experience:

> Black man, white man, Coloured man, European and African and Asian, Jew and Christian and Hindu and Moslem, all had come to honour her memory—their hates and their fears . . . all for this moment forgotten. . . . As for me, I was overwhelmed. I was seeing a vision, which was never to leave me. . . . In that church one was able to see, beyond any possibility of doubt, that what this woman

had striven for was the highest and best kind of thing to strive for in a country like South Africa. I knew then that I would never again be able to think in terms of race and nationality. I was no longer a white person but a member of the human race.[10]

And so, following a path of service to others, at Diepkloof, for example, and in the work of the Anglican Synod, a path illuminated by encounters with such persons as Mrs. Jones, Paton found his own way out of the dark wood. He created one metaphor for this journey of becoming a true South African in the character and writings of Arthur Jarvis, the murdered man in *Cry, the Beloved Country* who envisions an ideal society for South Africa.

Set over against Arthur Jarvis's intellectual quest, and transcending it, is the spiritual aspect of the quest of the chief pilgrim in this novel, Stephen Kumalo. Through its association with St. Stephen, the first Christian martyr who was cruelly stoned to death, Stephen Kumalo's name implies the way of suffering. Thus Paton created another metaphor, this time for the Christian journey, in the character and quest of Stephen Kumalo who, on the physical level, searches for his lost son, and on the intellectual level seeks to understand what must be done to restore society, and, finally, on a spiritual level, faces the temptation of despair before going forward in faith to endure the pain of his son's fate.

Kumalo's vision of peace, like Dante's glimpse of Paradise, cannot be reached on the earthly journey. Paton makes this clear in *For You Departed,* his memorial to his first wife, where, alluding to the vision of Isaiah, he says of *Cry, the Beloved Country:* "It is a song of love for one's far distant country, it is informed with longing for that land where they shall not hurt or destroy in all that holy mountain, for that unattainable and ineffable land where there shall be no more death. . . ."[11] The fact that Paton quotes this statement in what is his final word on *Cry, the Beloved Country,* his author's note in the 1987 Collier Books edition, supports the view that the theme of a spiritual quest in the novel is a primary one.

The theme of white emancipation from inbred racial prejudice embodied to some degree in both Arthur and James Jarvis is a recurring one in all of Paton's work. In the years following his writing of *Cry, the Beloved Country,* Paton wrote three more major works having as their theme the personal journey out from darkness into light. The first of these was his great biography of Jan Hofmeyr, *South African Tragedy,* which delineates Hofmeyr's journey out from the constraints of Afrikaner racial attitudes to become the champion of liberal attitudes toward race in South Africa. The second was *Apartheid and the Archbishop,* his biography of Archbishop Geoffrey Clayton, which shows the archbishop surmounting conventional white attitudes to take a courageous stand against apartheid in defiance of the government. The third was his own autobiography, which alludes to Isaiah's vision in its title, *Towards the Mountain.* The second volume of his autobiography, published shortly after his death in 1988 at age eighty-five, is therefore logically titled *Journey Continued.* The underlying theme of all these works—the quest for emancipation from constraining darkness—is a constant one also throughout *Cry, the Beloved Country,* even up to its final words: "But when the dawn will come, of our emancipation, from the fear of bondage and the bondage of fear, why, that is a secret" (277).

chapter 5

Style, Language, Characters

At least as many readers were drawn to *Cry, the Beloved Country* by the freshness of its language and the pleasures of its rhythms as by its insights into social dilemmas and complex relations among races. They were struck by the simplicity of its language and the unusual qualities of its prose style. In contrast to the commonplace language of daily journalism they found Paton's language fresh and lively. They also found a story told with great economy of means: its dialogue spare and effective; its ideas greatly compressed and therefore conducive to aphorism, which we associate with proverbial wisdom. Because of these qualities, and also because its rhythms often depend on parallel phrases and repetition, the style of *Cry, the Beloved Country* has frequently been described as "biblical." There are some grounds for this description, even though it does not apply to the style of the novel as a whole, nor can it be assumed to be Paton's personal style.

As is the case with his second novel, *Too Late the Phalarope*, Paton employs a biblical style for the speech of certain characters in *Cry, the Beloved Country* and also for some instances of a narrator's voice, particularly when the voice is prophetic. This style is reminiscent of the widely known standard translation of the Bible, the Authorized Version. It is most marked in the speech and thought of the two clergymen whose first language is Zulu: the Reverend Stephen Kumalo and the Reverend Theophilus Msimangu. The language of these characters may seem all the more biblical because they frequently employ phrases, or echoes of phrases, from the Bible—a book in which they are deeply read, and much of which they know by heart. But Paton endows these characters with a sonorous and musical style, not merely because they are clergymen, but because they are speakers of Zulu—a language full of the music of sonorous vowels, caressed as it were by lips and tongue, as in the river's name ending in sounds like the cooing of mourning doves: "the Valley of the Umzimkulu."

In any consideration of the relative presence of biblical and Zulu elements in the style of *Cry, the Beloved Country,* one passage in particular may be of special interest. The setting of this passage is Ezenzeleni, a place for the rehabilitation and training of the blind. In the course of a religious service Msimangu reads verses from Isa. 42: 6–7, which an English translation renders as: "I, the Lord, have called thee in righteousness, and will hold thine hand, and will keep thee, and give thee for a covenant for the people, for a light to the Gentiles; to open the blind eyes, to bring out the prisoners from the dungeon, and them that sit in darkness out of the prison-house." Msimangu reads this passage not in English but in Zulu; and the reader of the novel experiences the scene through the consciousness of Kumalo who had not known that his friend had such a voice: "For the voice was of gold, and the voice had love for the words it was reading. The voice shook and beat and trembled, not as the voice of an old man shakes and beats and trembles, but as a deep hollow bell when it is struck. For it was not only a voice of gold, but it was the voice of a man whose heart was golden, reading from a book of golden words" (90). The style of this passage is obviously not directly derived from the Bible; but it employs the poetic devices of repetition and parallelism found in the Bible. It is therefore a purposeful literary creation and not a direct imitation.

In fact, Paton employs a number of different styles in *Cry, the Beloved Country,* particularly to distinguish his characters from one another. No doubt, the one that may first strike readers as having a flavor of originality is the evocation of the rhythms of Zulu speech that appears chiefly in the Kumalo's speech and thought and also in the dialogue among other African characters. By contrast, the speech of the white Johannesburg businessman, Harrison, is composed almost wholly of conventional clichés. He is shown as a man hidebound by prejudice, who parrots hackneyed ideas about "the native problem."

But Harrison is a minor character, and his language may go almost unnoticed while the pattern of speech with a marked poetic quality accorded to Kumalo, Msimangu, and other African characters generally becomes the dominant style associated with the book. Possibly because the novel was published first in the United States, the initial reviewers recognized and remarked on overtones of biblical language with which they were familiar. But not all reviewers missed the Zulu overtones. Margaret Carson Hubbard remarked in the New York *Herald Tribune*: "It is almost as if the author were translating from the Zulu, but without stumbling into the circumlocutions and inexactnesses of a translation."[1] Ultimately, it is unnecessary to distinguish between elements in the style that are biblical and elements derived from Zulu. Paton's view, as expressed in the novel, is that the language of the Bible and the Zulu language have much in common: "When the storm threatens, a man is afraid for his house, said Father Vincent in that symbolic language that is like the Zulu tongue. But when the house is destroyed there is something to do" (108).

The fullest exploration, to date, of Paton's English representation of the Zulu speech of his characters is that of J. M. Coetzee in the course of his 1988 study, *White Writing: On the Culture of Letters in South Africa*. Coetzee, himself an outstanding novelist who is also a linguistics expert, finds that Paton's creation of a language for his Zulu characters is typical of a process that Coetzee calls *transfer*, which he defines as "the rendering of (imagined) foreign speech in an English stylistically marked to remind the reader of the (imagined) foreign original."[2] He also finds that in its closeness to its historical roots and in its preference for parable over abstraction, Paton's Zulu "seems to belong to an earlier and more innocent era of human culture," because in the mouths of certain characters "the Zulu original implied by Paton's English is both unrelievedly simple . . . and formal to the point of stateliness."[3]

Coetzee's insistence—in a reference to Paton's use of the legal term *pro deo*—that "words do not bear their histories with them as part of their meaning,"[4] and his frequent employment of categories like "feudal," may imply a structuralist approach in some ways averse to Paton's more religious standpoint. In particular, Coetzee feels that the language in some passages he has chosen for analysis conveys "a certain naïveté, even childishness, which reflects on the quality of mind of its speaker and of Zulu speakers in general."[5] This generalization obviously does not apply to the mind of the most educated speaker of Zulu in the novel, the Johannesburg priest, Msimangu—a man with a deep philosophical bent and a clear logical mind whose secular hero is the sharp-witted philosopher and advocate of racial tolerance, Alfred Hoernlé. Coetzee overlooks this, but he does not similarly overlook another representative of an educated generation: the young agricultural expert, Napoleon Letsitsi.

In his summing up Coetzee poses a rhetorical question: "What, if anything, then, separates Paton from those writers of the 1930s and 1940s who, under one disguise or another, call for the movement of history to come to a halt, for economic, social, and personal relations in the South African countryside to freeze forever in feudal postures?" Replying in the same cumbersome jargon, and with a gratuitous implication that Paton regretted feudalism's passing, he says: "The answer is, that, with however much regret, Paton accepts that the economic, and hence the political, basis of feudalism has been eroded by demographic forces."[6] This, he says, is what Kumalo learns from the young agricultural expert, Napoleon Letsitsi, who tells him: "We can restore the valley for those who are here, but when the children grow up, there will again be too many" (268). "To this young man," says Coetzee, "Paton allots the last and most telling word."[7] Letsitsi's wise words are, indeed, telling, but they are hardly more telling, qualitatively, than Msimangu's earlier eloquent words on the inevitability of social change: "Something is happening that no Bishop can stop. . . . You cannot stop the world from going on" (25). Patently, Paton does not represent all characters who speak Zulu as simple-minded or naive.

To a considerable extent, the speech of the African characters in *Cry, the Beloved Country* is a recreation in English of the sound and syntax of spoken Zulu. In this respect Paton's stylistic achievement resembles what the playwright J. M. Synge achieved in his Irish dialect plays. In both cases the "dialect" is a poetic invention deriving primarily from the demands of their materials and the emotions embodied in the works.

Both Synge and Paton affirm the value of poetic qualities in literature in strikingly similar ways. Synge once declared, "In a good play every speech should be as fully flavored as a nut or an apple, and such speeches cannot be written by anyone who works among people who have shut their lips on poetry."[8] Paton, reflecting perhaps on the theme of his novel, has said: "If you write in terms of poetry, fears and inhibitions disappear."[9]

Of course not all of what may be called poetry is written in verse. There is a long tradition that classifies as "poetic" in the broad sense all works of imaginative creation that contain elements of lyric, dramatic, or epic narrative modes. Many works of modern fiction such as James Joyce's *Ulysses*—and even more obviously his *Finnegans Wake*—may be so classified. So may Paton's *Cry, the Beloved Country*, particularly if we remember W. B. Yeats's pithy definition of a poem. "A poem," said Yeats, "is an elaboration of the rhythms of common speech and their association with profound feeling."[10] Even in the daily life of ordinary people the presence of strong emotions heightens the language. That is why, in highly emotional circumstances, people resort to metaphor and call other people "names"—ugly names if the emotion is anger or hatred, affectionate names if the emotion is love.

When commentators on *Cry, the Beloved Country* refer to its style or to the speech of some of its characters as biblical, what they mean, stated in technical terms, is that the novelist employs some of the devices of Hebrew poetry that are characteristic of various parts of the Bible.

The commonest devices used as aids to memory in Hebrew poetry are not devices of rhyme and metrical measurement as in English poetry; instead, they are those of parallelism and repetition highlighting the symmetry of ideas and images. (These are the biblical devices most apparent in the oratorical style of Martin Luther King, Jr., for example.) As already noted, a similar use of parallelism and repetition is common in the speech of some characters in *Cry, the Beloved Country*—as, for example, in Kumalo's description of Msimangu's voice as he preached at Ezenzeleni.

Another device of Hebrew poetry to be found in *Cry, the Beloved Country* is that of apostrophe, in which someone or something is directly addressed—for example, the country, South Africa, is addressed in the passage from which the novel takes its title: "Cry, the beloved country for the unborn child that is the inheritor of our fear. Let him not love the earth too deeply" (79). Yet another device of Hebrew poetry commonly found in *Cry, the Beloved Country* is that of aphorism—usually a brief assertion of truth or a "wise saying" that seems to have universal relevance. The most frequently noted instance in the novel is Msimangu's remark: "I have one great fear in my heart, that one day when they are turned to loving, they will find we are turned to hating" (40). This last quotation also illustrates how Paton's writing in *Cry, the Beloved Country* frequently rings prophetic, as does the Hebrew poetry of the Bible that is intimately linked with prophecy.

Writing that has the ring of prophecy is produced under the stress of powerful emotion—witness the zeal of the Old Testament prophets. Paton admits in his first volume of autobiography, *Towards the Mountain*, that *Cry, the Beloved Country* was so written: "I wrote for three days in Gothenburg under the influence of this powerful emotion. It continued to possess me for three months longer. I do not expect, and for a long time have not expected, to be revisited by it."[11] Such emotion, Paton feels, cannot be simulated or manufactured at will. In a poem on this subject, first published in 1961, he says that the words do not come out of nothing or form themselves into meanings unless some price has been paid for them:

Unless some deep thing is felt that runs
Like a living flame through their shapes and forms
So that . . . the pen
Smokes in the hand,
. . . and the paper chars
Under the heat of composition.[12]

Some critics may question the efficacy of emotion in a writer's work or fault him for not keeping proper distance from his subject. But there is ample testimony to the contrary from outstanding writers whose views support Paton in this regard. The Nobel Laureate, Boris Pasternak, says in his *Essay in Autobiography* that he believes the most astounding discoveries of all have been made at moments when the sense of his work so possessed the artist that it left him no time to think. Pasternak felt that, at such a time, the writer was "driven by his urgency to speak new words in the old language." Closer to home, the American novelist Peter Taylor, on receiving the 1987 Ritz-Hemingway Prize, said: "A serious writer must write out of compulsion." And he added: "I am suspicious of professionalism, which I have always felt comes perilously close to commercialism."[13]

It is not only in its emotional power, or in its evocation of those aspects of Hebrew poetry found in good translations of the Bible, that the style of *Cry, the Beloved Country* attains to the intensity of poetry. As implied earlier, the novel may be classified stylistically with those modern works of fiction that, like Joyce's *Ulysses,* have the intensity, compression, and connotative power of poetry in one or more of its three forms: lyric, dramatic, and narrative.

In its various parts and for differing purposes *Cry, the Beloved Country* employs the mode of poetry in its lyric, dramatic, and narrative forms. Lyric poetry is a form of expression related to the spontaneous impulses to sing and to dance for joy; or to the contrary impulses to mourn, bewail, or weep. Even when removed from the original impulse through embodiment in some conventional form such as the sonnet, lyric poetry is almost always felt to be, in some degree, incantatory. This quality of song is manifest in Paton's opening lyric passage (and others like it): "There is a lovely road that runs from Ixopo into the hills. These hills are grass-covered and rolling, and they are lovely beyond any singing of it" (3).

Paton has said in his autobiography, *Towards the Mountain,* that besides his early intense response to words and language, his childhood was marked by an intense awakening to nature: "I cannot describe my early response to the beauty of hill and stream and tree as anything less than ecstasy." He goes on to speak of his childhood delight in the colorful flowers of the Natal countryside. Some of these are named as seen from the train as Kumalo begins his journey: "the blue agapanthus, the wild watsonia, the red-hot poker . . . an aurum in the dell" (11). But the sound of birdcalls delighted him even more than these sights; and he goes so far as to say that some lines of Robert Louis Stevenson's "expressed my deepest feelings":

> Be it granted to me to behold you again in dying,
> Hills of home! and to hear again the call;
> Hear about the graves of the martyrs the peewees crying,
> And hear no more at all.[14]

Paton identifies the peewee, or peewit, as a member of the plover family. Another member of the plover family is the bird known in South Africa as the titihoya, whose plaintive anthem echoes through the opening chapter of *Cry, the Beloved Country* under discussion here: "About you there is grass and bracken and you may hear the forlorn cry of the titihoya, one of the birds of the veld. . . . But the rich green hills break down. . . . The titihoya does not cry there any more" (3).

The contrasting landscapes in this lyrical prelude to the novel—the carefully tended, rich green hills above and the eroded, overpopulated tribal lands below—provide a metaphor, or symbolic equivalent, for the main theme of the novel: the contrast between white well-being and black desolation in South African society as a whole. Whether this arrangement in the prelude is intentionally symbolic may be arguable; but that is not the case with certain other symbolic elements in the novel, such as the significance of the names of some major characters. The wayward boy, Absalom, for example, named after the son of King David in the Bible, is the son who causes his father much suffering, although, ironically, the name itself means "his father's peace." Stephen Kumalo, the father (and a Christian priest), takes his name, as stated earlier, from the first Christian who suffered martyrdom for his faith; and he too undergoes a kind of martyrdom, but still he steadfastly bears witness. The other dedicated priest, Theophilus Msimangu, takes his name from the New Testament. The Greek name *Theophilus* means "lover of God"; and it is, therefore, in keeping with his name that Msimangu should give up his possessions and enter a monastery. It is their behavior, not the mere chance of similarity, that proclaims symbolic kinship with a forerunner, or prototype, for the characters who bear these names. No such firm confirmation can be advanced to support Sheridan Baker's assumption that the name *Jarvis* is symbolically related to *Jaweh* or *Jehovah*.

While the allegorical significance of the names of a number of Paton's characters may be of some interest, the characters themselves are even more interesting as psychological types. Almost all of them have mysterious depths and varying degrees of inner turmoil, as is the case also with the characters in his second novel, *Too Late the Phalarope*. It seems probable that some of the psychological insight Paton brought to the development of characters in his novels may have come from formal study of psychological works for the degree of master of education or in preparation for undertaking his work at Diepkloof Reformatory. Besides the basic works of Freud, Montessori, A. S. Neill, and John Dewey, these included, in particular, William McDougall's *Abnormal Psychology,* and also a book that Paton says changed the direction of his life: Cyril Burt's *The Young Delinquent.*

But for the rounding out of his characters and the representation of their inner contradictions, Paton went beyond his formal studies. He has said that much of what he discovered about the complexity of human nature came not only from books but from life experience. In an autobiographical essay written in the mid-1960s for a symposium titled "What I Have Learned," which appeared in the *Saturday Review*, Paton says that his discovery of the complexity of human nature was accompanied by another discovery—the discovery of the complexity and irrationality of human motives: "the discovery that one could love and hate simultaneously, be honest and cheat, be arrogant and humble, be any pair of opposites that one had supposed to be mutually exclusive." He adds that although the complexity and irrationality of human motives is not common knowledge, and is even incomprehensible to many, "it has always been known, of course, by the dramatists and novelists. It is, in fact, a knowledge far more disturbing to other people than to writers, for to writers it is the grist to their mills."[15] And it is certainly grist to Paton's mill.

Despite the allegorical significance of some of their names, Paton's characters in *Cry, the Beloved Country* are not representative types but, rather, unique individuals. Stephen Kumalo, for example, does not represent a white stereotype of a black African—though some have chosen to see him that way; nor is the young reformatory worker who handles Absalom's case a white Afrikaner stereotype. Each is torn, at times, by contradictory impulses; and, as is the case with all significant characters in literature, the more one gets to know them, the more memorable they become. So also do the other characters in *Cry, the Beloved Country*: those with larger roles like Msimangu, Absalom Kumalo, James Jarvis, and John Kumalo; and those with lesser roles like Gertrude, the Harrisons, Absalom's girl, and the young agricultural expert, Napoleon Letsitsi.

The allegorical element in the names of some characters may bring to *Cry, the Beloved Country* a certain flavor of medieval morality plays; but the symbolism of names is not the point at which the novel comes closest to drama. The sure and effective handling of dialogue in *Cry, the Beloved Country* shows a considerable maturity in dramatic writing. Such a skill does not come automatically; it is acquired and developed over time. Besides writing verse as a young man, Paton also attempted at least two poetic dramas that were produced by the dramatic society at Natal University College. Although slight and amusing pieces, they show that he aspired early to dramatic writing. The passages of dialogue in *Cry, the Beloved Country*—and they are extensive—show a considerable mastery of at least one dramatic technique familiar to playwrights.

In Greek drama, at moments of highest emotion, the speech of the characters frequently takes the form of short, sharp alternating lines or half-lines of dialogue, characterized by the thrust and parry of contrasting statements and by echoing repetition of words and phrases. This form of dialogue, known technically as *stichomythia,* was introduced into English and used effectively by Elizabethan playwrights including Shakespeare. Take, for example, the well-known passage of give and take between Hamlet and his mother, with its reversals and repetition:

> "Now, Mother, what's the matter?"
> "Hamlet, thou hast thy father much offended."
> "Mother, you have my father much offended."
> "Come, come, you answer with an idle tongue."
> "Go, go, you question with a wicked tongue." (3. 4. 8–12)

There is an approximation of this kind of dialogue—except, of course, that the humble speakers do not have Hamlet's rapierlike wit—in passages like the following:

> "Have you a house for me yet?"
> "There is no house yet."
> "Are you sure my name is on the list?"
> "Yes, your name is on the list."
> "What number am I on the list?" (54–55)

These instances of dramatically effective dialogue are not intended to imply that Paton intentionally chose Greek or Elizabethan dramatists as models; but, rather, they illustrate that in all dramatic speech, especially when the emotion is intense, the dialogue is appropriately terse and rapid. The great modern poet W. B. Yeats, for example, recognized this when he set himself the ideal of writing poetic drama "where every speech would be short and concentrated, knit by dramatic tension."[16] Paton's style in *Cry, the Beloved Country* tends to approximate effective drama, and particularly poetic drama, in this regard. Among the more notable instances of heightened dramatic tension in the novel are the passages of hurried dialogue toward the end of chapter 12; the prison encounters between father and son in chapters 16 and 17; and the meeting between the two fathers in chapter 25.

Even in those chapters of *Cry, the Beloved Country* whose purpose would appear to be wholly narrative—such as chapter 9 on the building of Shanty Town or chapter 23 on the effects of the discovery of new gold—Paton employs artistic devices that give the heightened effect of poetry. Each of these chapters brings together a number of separate little dramatic vignettes into a kind of collage. This artistic device, as in a film sequence where the camera focuses rapidly on separate but related events, serves to heighten the pace and intensify interest. It may be seen at its most dramatic in the sequence in chapter 12 during which the two priests, Msimangu and Kumalo, hurry from place to place in search of Absalom but always remain one step behind the police.

Even though the action in *Cry, the Beloved Country* is represented largely through dialogue as in a play, there is also significant reliance on the voice of an omniscient narrator speaking from outside the action. The method of transfer from the narrative mode to the dramatic is established at the outset. After the narrator's lyrical prologue on the rich green hills and the nearby desolate valleys, the focus shifts to the specific details of village life in the valley as the little girl runs with the letter to the priest's house. Book 2 opens in a similar manner. In this case when the lyric voice breaks off—as it does, appropriately, at the end of the "white" segment—the scene moves to High Place where James Jarvis is supervising the plowing of his drought-baked fields. Once established, this method permits easy alternation between narrative and dramatic modes as occasion may require; and it allows the lyric voice to reenter at moments of high emotion, as in the obvious case of those passages from which the novel takes its title.

Such alternation of narrative and dramatic sequences is fairly common in fiction, particularly in the work of writers like John Steinbeck and Ernest Hemingway, both of whom are masters of the technique of storytelling through dialogue. But there is one marked difference in the case of *Cry, the Beloved Country.* Here Paton resorts to a narrative voice not merely to complement the dramatic method. He employs a number of narrative voices, one of which is both omniscient and markedly poetic. It may be said that Paton, a writer of both poetry and drama, effectively combined aspects of his talent for both modes of expression in his novel.

It may be pertinent, in this regard, to recall two plays of the 1930s written in collaboration by the poet W. H. Auden and the novelist Christopher Isherwood. In the case of these two plays, *The Dog beneath the Skin* and *The Ascent of F6,* Isherwood provided most of the dramatic dialogue for scenes that carried the plot forward. Auden composed prologues in verse and other verse interludes that function almost like opera arias. In Paton's hands, the omniscient lyric voice in *Cry, the Beloved Country* functions in an approximately equivalent way to Auden's verse in the collaborations with Isherwood. The method of Paton's novel, a narrative combining lyric and dramatic modes, is both unusual and successful in this respect.

It should be no surprise to find poetic qualities in a serious novel that has sometimes been described as a novel of social protest. When such protest is grounded in deeply felt experience, and when the writer is sufficiently skilled, the intensity of feeling will often demand expression in a dramatic or poetic medium. This was the case with a number of novels—all of them at one time or another described by critics as "novels of social protest"—that had attracted Paton prior to his writing of *Cry, the Beloved Country.* These novels also have in common a background of a rural landscape that powerfully influences the lives of the characters.

Paton's interest in such novels of significant social setting began very early. Awarded a literary prize as a schoolboy, he chose as his award a collection of the novels of Charles Dickens. Later, as a schoolmaster, he had attempted to write two novels of South African farm life set in Natal; he was influenced, he felt, by Hugh Walpole's popular novels of middle-class life, *Rogue Herries* (1930) and *Judith Paris* (1931), which were set in, or near, the English Lake District.

In fact, the landscapes behind works of literature always appealed to his imagination. At age twenty-four he had his first opportunity to visit England as a delegate to an international student conference representing the students of Natal University College. He took advantage of this opportunity to tour England and Scotland, chiefly by motorcycle, visiting the Lake District and other places of literary interest. In one of his reports to the students in Natal—alluding to places associated with Wordsworth, A. E. Housman, and Shakespeare—he said: "Poetic enthusiasts will writhe when I say I spent some time in the ruins of Tintern Abbey, slept a night at Ludlow, and am this afternoon going to Stratford."

To return to the group of novels of social protest—chiefly of the 1930s—that may in a general way have some bearing on Paton's style in *Cry, the Beloved Country,* it is clear that the most immediate was John Steinbeck's *The Grapes of Wrath.* Paton first read this novel—an account of the efforts of a farming family from the dust bowl of the West to reach the "promised land" of California—while he was in Stockholm, very shortly before beginning his own novel. Paton says that the experience of reading *The Grapes of Wrath* made a deep impression on him, and in some sense it "triggered" his urge to write; but he adds that Steinbeck was not an influence on his own writing, even though he did adopt "his style of rendering conversations, indicating by a preliminary dash that a speech was about to begin, and omitting all inverted commas."[17]

Another novel of the 1930s that was probably more influential on Paton's style is *Sunset Song,* the first novel of a trilogy called *A Scots Quair* by the Scottish writer James Leslie Mitchell, who wrote under the pen name Lewis Grassic Gibbon. Gibbon writes of the struggles of a woman on an isolated Scottish farm through the period of World War I and the Great Depression, and he does so in a style that has been described as "a powerful, idiosyncratic lyrical prose." Gibbon also employs a form of Scots dialect that may have suggested to Paton a manner of handling the speech of his Zulu characters.

The last of these significant novels is by the Norwegian novelist, Knut Hamsun, who was awarded the Nobel Prize in literature in 1920. Isaac Bashevis Singer, himself a Nobel laureate in 1978, wrote in his commentary, "Knut Hamsun: Artist of Skepticism,": "The whole modern school of fiction in the twentieth century stems from Hamsun"— and this despite the fact that Hamsun in his old age showed support for Adolf Hitler after his invasion of Norway.[18] It was Hamsun's early novel, *Growth in the Soil,* that so greatly attracted Paton's attention that he undertook his side trip to Norway for the express purpose of visiting its setting—a journey spurred by the same interest in literary landscape that twenty years earlier had brought him to Tintern Abbey and Ludlow and Stratford-upon-Avon. Even though he discovered Knut Hamsun's reputation to be tarnished by his later politics, Paton's literary pilgrimage to Norway turned out to be a fruitful one.

chapter 6

Stephen Kumalo:
The Quest

Paton says he began writing *Cry, the Beloved Country* under the influence of a deep emotion that was partly the longing for home. On 24 September 1946 he had set out by train from Stockholm, Sweden, to visit the Norwegian countryside where Knut Hamsun had set his novel *Growth in the Soil*. Through the night and all the next day his train traveled through mountainous border country, a land of pine forests and waterfalls. This northern countryside close to the Arctic Circle was wholly unlike the rolling hills of Paton's beloved landscape of Natal, so far away, south of the equator, on the east coast of southern Africa.

Toward evening on 25 September Paton arrived at the Hotel Bristol, in Trondheim, where he had difficulty communicating with a receptionist who knew no English. A local resident, an engineer named Jensen, came to his assistance. Jensen later showed Paton Trondheim's cathedral with its fine stained-glass rose window. As they sat contemplating the beautiful window in the late evening light, Paton became increasingly aware of a strong emotion that had been growing in him all day while he watched the strange new landscape passing by. Jensen showed Paton back to the Hotel Bristol and promised to return in an hour to take him to dinner. In that hour, in the grip of a powerful emotion that was not directly related to the cathedral or the rose window but, nevertheless, as he says in *Towards the Mountain,* "occasioned by them," Paton sat in his hotel room and composed the lyric passages that were to become the opening chapter of his novel.

The emotion that gripped Paton that September evening in Trondheim was in great part an intense homesickness for his wife and his sons and also for his far-off country. It is not too surprising, therefore, that his opening lines—"There is a lovely road that runs from Ixopo into the hills. These hills are grass-covered and rolling, and they are lovely beyond any singing of it" (3)—should recall a place dear to him: not only because he thought the landscape beautiful but also because it was the place where as a young man he had his first teaching post, where he first fell in love, and where he was married.

At age twenty-two, following his graduation from Natal University College and his return from representing the students of that college at the Imperial Student Conference in England, Paton took up the post of teacher of mathematics and physics at Ixopo High School—a school for white children. (The many accounts of Paton that say he went to Ixopo to teach black children—even including his obituary in the London *Times* of 13 April 1988—are mistaken on this point.) While teaching at Ixopo Paton began to fall in love with a young married woman, Doris Olive Francis, whose husband, Bernard Lusted, was dying of tuberculosis. A year or so after Bernard's death they were married in St. John's Anglican Church in Ixopo on 2 July 1928.

While teaching at Ixopo and later at Pietermaritzburg, Paton had attempted two or three novels of white South African life set among farms like those of his wife's relatives in the rich green hills of Natal. But now, from the perspective of Trondheim, after the years of involvement with black lives at Diepkloof and the vision of a nonracial society that had come to him through his work for the Anglican Church Synod in Johannesburg, he saw the remembered landscape differently. The opening lyric passage—in essence an ode to the landscape—does not end with the evocation of the rich soil of well-kept white farms on the higher lands. In the manner of the classical Greek ode with its opening strophe and its counterturn into the contrasting antistrophe, the passage turns to survey the poor, eroded, red soil draining like life's blood from the overpopulated and overgrazed land of the African reserves below.

This contrast of richness and poverty in the lyric opening supplies a leitmotiv for the vision of the two contrasting worlds of white and black South Africa that follows in the novel as a whole. The destruction of the soil foreshadows social destruction: "The rich green hills break down"; and the titihoya—the plover-like bird with the mournful cry—"does not cry there any more." In the eroded valleys of the black reserves, only the old and the children remain to scratch out a living. The young men and the young girls have gone away. Appropriately, it is a child and an old couple, the Zulu pastor Stephen Kumalo and his wife, that the reader first meets. In his autobiography, Paton says there was no weighty reason in his choice of a humble black priest; it was just that he remembered that such a man used to visit his delinquent son at Diepkloof and counsel him to prepare for a law-abiding life. This old man wore his minister's clothing and made no attempt to hide the fact that a clergyman had such a son.

In the novel, the story of the Reverend Stephen Kumalo begins in his home in the small, isolated Zululand village of Ndotsheni where he is pastor of the local Anglican church constructed of wood and tin. There are no amenities in the village: no postal deliveries, no stores. A little girl brings a letter from the only place the postal service recognizes, the white man's store further away. The letter is from Johannesburg, the distant city to which all the impoverished villagers are attracted to seek work. Stephen Kumalo's brother, John, has gone there. The husband of his sister, Gertrude, went there and was not heard from again. She went there to look for him and did not return. His son, Absalom, then went there to look for Gertrude and he too is no longer heard from. A letter from such a place addressed in unknown handwriting can be thought to bring only bad news, and Kumalo and his wife fear to open it. The striking of this note of fear introduces a theme that resonates throughout the novel: "Have no doubt there is fear in the land" (75).

The letter from Johannesburg is dated 25 September 1946. Besides coinciding with the date on which Paton began to write the novel, this date, together with the dates of subsequent events such as the trial, sets the historical moment of the novel's events in the year 1946. The letter does not bring news of Absalom; but it does bring news of Gertrude. It informs Kumalo that she is very sick, and it recommends that he should come to Johannesburg to care for her.

Although the news is bad, the letter brings some glimmer of hope. This hope derives from the impression the letter conveys of the character and personality of the writer who is a fellow priest: the Reverend Theophilus Msimangu of the Mission House, Sophiatown, Johannesburg. Msimangu is clearly a man of compassion who offers brotherly assistance. As we come to know him in the course of the novel he is sophisticated, eloquent, well-read, and wise in the ways of the city.

Stephen Kumalo, by contrast, is none of these things; but neither is he uneducated nor lacking in intellect. He is a simple man, learned in his own calling—as we see when the little girl who brings the letter is amazed to see all the books in his house: "more even than the books at the school" (5). As a character in a novel, Kumalo is akin to a character type commonly met in European literature: the rural pastor of France or Italy, for example, who is rich in the virtues of humility and goodness while lacking in city sophistication. The inner strengths of Kumalo's character will become apparent in the course of the novel as event after event adds to his suffering. Meanwhile it may be said that he is by no means a white man's stereotype of a backward African, as a few critics have implied. Neither is he portrayed as a saint; he has human failings that master him occasionally.

The anxiety aroused in him by the letter's news of Gertrude, and by its lack of news of his son or his brother, expresses itself in frustrated bitterness. His wife feels the edge of his anger as she encourages him to take the money they had saved for Absalom's education at St. Chad's School. (From its English patron's name we assume it to be an

Anglican institution.) Kumalo's resentment is fueled by the reminder that his dearest wish of a good education for his son seems now a forlorn hope. But he agrees to go the next day; he apologizes to his wife for hurting her with his sharpness; and, as he does in desolate moments throughout the novel, he goes to pray alone. "It was in this world alone that he was certain" (14), says the narrator when Kumalo takes out his sacred book on the train next day.

Kumalo is no less fearful and anxious as he begins his long train journey the next morning. The train rides through the night "over battlefields of long ago" (15) and over the escarpment separating coastal Natal from the high interior plains. The "battlefields of long ago" would include those of the 1830s, when the white Afrikaner voortrekkers fought off Zulu power at the Battle of the Blood River, for instance, and established their Republic of the Transvaal in which there would be by law "no equality in church or state" between black and white inhabitants. The battlefields would also include those of the Boer War (1899–1901) between Boer armies from the Transvaal and British armies based in Natal. The plains of the Transvaal, known as the high veld, "rolling away as far as the eye can see" (15), are new and strange to Kumalo who has always lived in the part of Natal known as the Valley of a Thousand Hills. Strange to him also, as "a Zulu schooled in English," is the language of the Transvaal which he sees on railroad signs. This is the language "called Afrikaans, a language he had never yet heard spoken" (15). Kumalo fears the unknown world of Johannesburg. He recalls that a boy from his village was killed crossing the street there. He is oppressed by "the fear of Gertrude's sickness" and, "deep down, the fear of his son"; and he also experiences the more universal fear of a man uprooted from a familiar tribal way of life: "the fear of a man who lives in a world not made for him, whose own world is slipping away, dying, being destroyed, beyond any recall" (14).

This is Kumalo's uneasy sense of the world of South Africa and of his place in it as he sets out on his quest. If there is to be significant development in his character as the action of the novel unfolds, we must expect that this initial vision will be altered or greatly expanded by his tribulations. At one level of experience he must come to terms with the problems of his family: his son, sister, and brother; and at another level he must respond to the plight of his people in their changing world. But in any full consideration of Kumalo as a literary character it is necessary to recognize that he is not a man of action such as a soldier or politician who is judged by his public deeds. Nor is he a creative artist who is judged by the quality of his work. As we are constantly reminded, he is a clergyman of the Anglican Church whose ultimate duty is faithfulness to his priestly calling. This adds a third level of interest to his character—a spiritual dimension not commonly found in the genre described as "novels of social protest," such as *The Grapes of Wrath.*

That is why F. Charles Rooney can say the following about Paton's *Cry, the Beloved Country:* "He searches the dilemma of man's fear and disregard for his fellows with all the compassion and force of Steinbeck in *The Grapes of Wrath.* Yet he has what Steinbeck never had, a vision of the life of the spirit. He has all Steinbeck's heart, plus *soul.*" Rooney adds that, for Paton, "love, supernatural forgiving love, is the imperative of life; without it life is destroyed. It is the vacuum created by fear and hate that is the cause of all conflict in his novels; his insight into this void has set Paton's novels not only beyond but on a different plane from the bulk of modern fiction."[1]

Cry, the Beloved Country is divided into three books. These may be thought of as corresponding in a general way to the three stages of Kumalo's quest: the physical, the intellectual, and the spiritual. In book 1, Kumalo is primarily occupied with his search for his sister and his son. In the course of this search he journeys anxiously from place to place in the city following a succession of leads, and he suffers anguish and deep desolation bordering on despair. In book 2, which is more properly the book of the white father and son, James and Arthur Jarvis, Kumalo comes to terms with his son's tragedy and with his own responsibility for what remains of his son's family. In book 3 he accepts an increasing measure of responsibility for restoring the land and the people. He also endures a spiritual crisis and finds reconciliation.

Stephen Kumalo: The Quest

To begin with, the simple, fearful man, Stephen Kumalo, travels to the unfamiliar industrial world of Johannesburg. His experiences there open his eyes to various manifestations of good and evil in the new urban society. Before reaching the Mission House in Sophiatown where the helpful Zulu priest, Msimangu, is waiting for him, he is first robbed by one fellow African, then treated with sympathy and consideration by another. Later, Msimangu brings him to places of desolation like the Claremont slum where he finds his sister, Gertrude, now a prostitute; and to places of hope like Ezenzeleni where the blind are rehabilitated. He becomes aware of his brother John's self-seeking corruption and of Msimangu's selfless generosity. And he witnesses something he was even less prepared for: the commitment of some of his own people to bettering the lot of the desperately poor. This group included men like Dubula who organize both the bus boycott and the building of the squatters' Shanty Town.

Kumalo also becomes more conscious of the conflicting impulses in his own temperament. He is "the good pastor" seeking lost sheep; yet he lies to his fellow travelers on the train to protect his self-esteem. He is cruelly angry with the nameless girl who is to bear Absalom's child; and, with greater reason, he is cruelly angry with his brother, John, whose cunning has saved his own son at Absalom's expense.

The themes of the desolated land and the broken tribe first raised in the lyric prelude are further orchestrated upon Kumalo's arrival at the Mission House in Sophiatown. There Kumalo shares a meal with Msimangu and his fellow Anglican priests both black and white, including the rosy-cheeked priest from England, Father Vincent. When their conversation turns to the place Kumalo came from, he tells them "of the sickness of the land, of the broken tribe, of the broken house, of young men and young girls that went away and forgot their customs" (22). They, in turn, tell him of the wave of crime in Johannesburg.

After dinner Msimangu takes Kumalo aside and tells him, sympathetically, of Gertrude's "sickness"—her prostitution and illicit liquor selling—and of her child growing up in that environment. In a series of passages of well-managed dialogue their conversation moves on to other topics of urgent concern to Kumalo: his fears for his son, Absalom, whom Msimangu does not know; and for his brother, John, of whom Msimangu says, "He has no use for the church any more" (26). When Kumalo wonders what his bishop will say when he hears about this family of one of his priests, Msimangu says that something is happening that no bishop can stop, something that "must go on."

When Kumalo expresses shock at hearing this, Msimangu responds with one of the key arguments in the novel—an argument that we meet again in Arthur Jarvis's essays in book 2. These things must go on, Msimangu says, because you cannot stop the world from going on: "The tragedy is not that things are broken. The tragedy is that they are not mended again. . . . It suited the white man to break the tribe, . . . But it has not suited him to build something in place of what is broken" (26). Msimangu's recognition that the old tribal way cannot be restored, that you cannot stop the world from going on, is diametrically opposed to the beliefs of those whites, principally Afrikaners, who in the year that the novel was published introduced the system known as apartheid. This system sought retribalization by demanding that Africans, instead of sharing a common citizenship with whites, should develop separately "along their own lines" in designated tribal areas called "homelands." At the time that Paton wrote *Cry, the Beloved Country* it seemed that only an extremist splinter group of the Afrikaner Nationalist party held such a view. Therefore, in the novel, their view is represented merely as one view among a number of others that clamor for attention among the medley of white voices in chapter 12: "And some cry for the cutting up of South Africa without delay into separate areas, where white can live without black, and black without white" (78).

While the novel gives no premonition of this turn of events in white politics, it does offer a glimpse of how the political methods of African nationalism might evolve in the cities in opposition to white Afrikaner nationalism. In this regard Kumalo's quest for his son is also a fruitful technical device. It not only retains our interest in what Kumalo endures in the private matter of his lost son, but it also introduces us to the public world of black urban society. It is chiefly in the course of Kumalo's successive journeys from the Mission House in Sophiatown to such varied African townships as Claremont, Alexandra, Orlando, and nearby Shanty Town that we see the prospect of future political events unfolding from an African perspective.

One way in which Paton opens up this perspective to our view is through the instrumentality of his guide, Msimangu. Another is through a series of glimpses of the work of those committed to a variety of social or political causes. Among those motivated by a social conscience are Msimangu and his fellow priests at the Mission House, the staff of the institute for the blind at Ezenzeleni, and the staff of the reformatory, both black and white, who are concerned with Absalom's welfare. But beyond these more conventional workers for social justice, *Cry, the Beloved Country* introduces a relatively new theme in South African literature: the beginnings of black activist politics in urban areas. The politically motivated include: Kumalo's brother, John; "a brown man" named Tomlinson whom we do not meet; and Dubula who organizes the boycott of the buses to Alexandra and the building of Shanty Town overnight near Orlando. Msimangu says of Dubula: "They say that Tomlinson has the brains, and your brother the voice, but that this man has the heart" (43).

The journey that opens Kumalo's eyes to what is happening in Johannesburg, beyond the immediate tribulations of his own family, is an arduous one; and its very arduousness offers much insight into the heavy burden placed on blacks simply by the mechanics of a framework of segregation. The Johannesburg metropolitan area at the time of the novel's setting may be thought of as circular in shape approximating a wheel. The main railroad station at which Kumalo arrived and the nearby business and financial district formed the hub. This central business district was ringed, further out, by white residential suburbs, of which the wealthier had parks and golf courses. Further out still, beyond the white suburbs, lay the segregated townships where black people lived. This arrangement imposed an extra burden of travel on blacks who worked in the city and also an added expense.

Later, in the 1950s, when theorists of apartheid imposed the separate "homelands" policies, some black workers were faced with bus journeys of several hours each way daily.

Travel from one black township to another in the vicinity of the city posed another problem. The main roads and all public transport lines radiated out from the central Johannesburg hub like the spokes of a wheel. Therefore a journey from one black township like Sophiatown, where Kumalo lodged with Mrs. Lithibe, to another satellite township like Alexandra usually required a double journey—in to the central hub and then out again. Sophiatown and Claremont, where Kumalo finds Gertrude, were fairly close together, five or six miles west of the city center. Orlando and Shanty Town lay about eight miles southwest of the city hub. Pimville, where Absalom's girl lives, was about three miles further to the southwest. Alexandra (named, no doubt, for the wife of England's King Edward VII), where Absalom once lodged with Mrs. Mkize, was directly across the metropolitan area to the northeast, eleven miles from the central hub on a bus route that Kumalo finds boycotted by black workers who choose to walk because they cannot afford a fare increase.

Kumalo and Msimangu cross and recross this whole metropolitan area for several days as they seek out Kumalo's sister, Gertrude; his brother, John; and, principally, his son, Absalom. At times they travel on foot; at other times, by bus; at times of dire need, by taxi; and once, because of the bus boycott, they get a ride from a white driver sympathetic to the striking workers. Kumalo's extensive quest serves the novelist as a useful technical device that introduces the reader to the world of the African townships as his rural clergyman experiences this world directly and also as he learns about it indirectly through his well-informed guide, Msimangu.

On his first day in Johannesburg Kumalo learns of widespread urban crime and moral degeneration from his own brush with petty thievery and from the dinner conversation with Msimangu and the other clergymen at the Sophiatown Mission House. On the second day he experiences shock at the filth of Claremont, "the garbage heap of the great city," where his sister's house is a place for prostitution and the sale of illicit liquor; but he has his first apparent success there when Gertrude agrees to take her little boy away from that environment and rejoin her family. On the third day he walks with Msimangu to his brother's house in another part of Sophiatown. He is disturbed to find his brother devious and greatly changed; but his hopes are raised when he learns that Absalom and his cousin have worked in the Doornfontein factory district directly across the city to the east. With Msimangu he hurries across the city to the factory only to find that Absalom is no longer employed there. The factory can supply only an address of a Mrs. Ndlela of End Street, Sophiatown, where Absalom and his cousin once had lodgings. When they journey back to Sophiatown they find that the only trace of the boys Mrs. Ndlela can supply is an address of a Mrs. Mkize in faraway Alexandra township.

The fourth day is physically and mentally even more trying. It is also the day on which Kumalo encounters the public manifestation of African discontent and political action. (What had been a matter of words in the mouth of his brother he now sees, in the bus boycott, as purposeful activity.) When he and Msimangu eventually reach Alexandra they get no information, at first, from the fearful and evasive Mrs. Mkize; but later she reluctantly admits to Msimangu that Absalom and his friends had brought many things to her house, and that they had left there because they were near to being discovered by the police. She also referred Msimangu to the taxi-driver, Hlabeni, who knew the boys. From the taxi-driver whom they hired to take them home because of the bus boycott, Kumalo and Msimangu learn that Absalom and his cousin had gone to live among the squatters of Shanty Town, and that the people there would know where to find them. As it was late in the day they were forced to return by taxi across the city to Sophiatown, and they agreed to wait until the next day before continuing their search for Absalom in Shanty Town.

The unfolding story of Kumalo's quest breaks off at this point for a choral episode, in chapter 9, comprising snatches of anonymous dialogue and brief confrontations between Africans seeking somewhere to live in the overcrowded townships. This choral episode widens the novel's perspectives on the broken tribes, on the tribulations of black migrants, and on the desperate plight of the black population generally. In doing so it intensifies the element of dramatic tension preparatory to the Shanty Town episode, which, as noted above, is the principal manifestation of black political activism in the novel; and preparatory, also, to the revelation that Absalom has had a record of arrest and conviction.

The Building of Shanty Town is the second instance of successful nonviolent protest organized by Dubula. In contrast to John Kumalo who "sits like a chief" comfortably at home and who likes the sound of his own voice, Dubula goes out into the streets and works quietly and unselfishly in practical ways to help his people. In the course of the bus boycott he avoids violence or intimidation and relies on moral persuasion. He approaches would-be passengers like Kumalo and Msimangu, and he asks them respectfully not to use the buses. His tactics, and those of the committee he leads to organize the homeless and have them set up Shanty Town overnight in the empty land by the railroad, are purposeful. Faced with a fait accompli and public response to newspaper pictures of the pitiful shanties—"What will the poor devils do in the rain? What will the poor devils do in the winter?"—the authorities are shamed into some kind of action: "Men come, and machines come, and they start building rough houses for us" (59).

During the night of the building of Shanty Town the private anguish of the woman from the rural areas whose baby is dying holds our interest in the foreground. Beyond her personal tragedy, the public organization of nonviolent resistance goes on. Outside she hears some of the other squatters singing around a fire. They are singing in Zulu the hymn, "God Save Africa": "*Nkosi Sikelel' iAfrika*." At the time in which the novel was set and written, the hymn "*Nkosi Sikelel' iAfrika*" would have been known to none beyond South Africa and only to a few of the white population there. These few would have included people like Paton who worked among African youths at Diepkloof Reformatory and those who worked at African schools or visited African schools or churches to hear the singing of choirs. What they heard sung in these places was not a song of defiance but a hymn that was hauntingly beautiful when sung in the African manner with a blending of voices.

During the half-century or so since then—a half-century in which the supporters of apartheid have held power—"*Nkosi Sikelel' iAfrika,*" like "We Shall Overcome" in America, came to be universally recognized as an anthem of protest. In *Cry, the Beloved Country* we hear the first stirrings of this protest in the voices of those who join the activist, Dubula, in setting up Shanty Town overnight. Toward the end of the novel, we hear it also in the words of the young black agricultural instructor who takes inspiration from "*Nkosi Sikelel' iAfrika.*" This young man represents a new generation with a patriotic loyalty to Africa. He grows excited as he tells Kumalo: "We work for Africa"; and when Kumalo asks why he does not say South Africa," he responds, "We would if we could." And he adds: "We speak as we sing . . . for we sing *Nkosi Sikelel' iAfrika*" (269).

Finally, with regard to black participation in political protest, it is evident that Paton's sympathies lie with Dubula, who seeks a more just dispensation through the moral strength of nonviolence, and not with John Kumalo who, if he had the courage, would seek political power through violent confrontation. In his methods of organization and protest, Dubula follows the example of Mahatma Gandhi who lived and worked for many years in South Africa. It was in South Africa during the early years of the twentieth century that Gandhi developed his methods of nonviolent resistance to injustice. Gandhi had even been confined in Diepkloof Prison—the place Paton later changed into a reform school—during 1913 for defying laws that denied Indians entry into the Transvaal. Throughout his political life Paton himself remained committed to nonviolence, which was the fundamental policy of the Liberal party. Toward the end of his life, adherence to this commitment separated him from those opponents of apartheid who lost hope in nonviolence and felt that violence was inevitable. The subject of his last novel, *Ah, but Your Land Is Beautiful* (1981), is the nonviolent resistance campaign of 1952 in South Africa.

In *Cry, the Beloved Country*, Dubula's political tactics of nonviolent protest, and of organizing Africans to depend on their own efforts to build shelters in Shanty Town, are prominent among the things that open Kumalo's eyes to something new that was occurring among his people. Later, when he comes to terms with his own tribulations, the memory of this experience encourages him to take a lead in seeking to change things when he returns to his village. But these eventualities are far in the future. The immediate consequence of Kumalo's visit to Shanty Town is another blow: the discovery that Absalom has had a record of arrest and conviction.

chapter 7

Stephen Kumalo: Desolation

When, on the fifth day of their search, Kumalo and Msimangu inquire about Absalom among the squatters in Shanty Town, they learn that he was taken away by police months earlier and sent to the nearby reform school. This news that his son has been tried and sentenced for criminal activity is a new blow to Kumalo, already dejected by the discovery that his sister is a prostitute and that his brother is a corrupt political agitator who has abandoned both his wife and the church. It is also a new cause for fear as, with Msimangu, he makes his way to the reform school to seek further information.

At first the reform school gives promise of ill fortune reversed and hope restored. A young white social worker takes obvious pride in telling them that Absalom had done well there—so well, in fact, that he was released a month before to enable him to work outside the reformatory and prepare to marry his pregnant girlfriend. The social worker seems quite certain of Absalom's reform. He speaks of good reports from the place where he found work for him and of his having saved three or four pounds in the post office savings account he encouraged him to open. While they wait for the young man to be free to take them to Pimville where Absalom and his girl live, they are given further cause for hope by a friendly black teacher who invites them to his house and tells them how Absalom had done well at the reformatory. (This character is based on Ben Moloi, the head teacher at Diepkloof; that of the white social worker is based on "Lanky" de Lange, a young Afrikaner who was exceptionally dedicated to the work of rehabilitating black delinquents.) But the hopes raised at the reform school are dashed when they arrive at the girl's place in Pimville. The girl tells them that Absalom is missing, and this is confirmed by the factory where he worked.

That evening during dinner with the priests at the Mission House in Sophiatown the talk turns again to the problem of crime. Someone produces a newspaper with the latest headlines. A well-known city engineer has been shot dead in his home by assailants "thought to be Natives." The victim, Arthur Jarvis, is known to the white priest, Father Vincent, as a great fighter for justice. He is known to Msimangu as president of the Claremont African Boys Club. And Kumalo recognizes the name as that of the only son of James Jarvis from the farm High Place, near Ndotsheni. Father Vincent reads aloud the newspaper account of the killing of a man "known for his interest in social problems" who is now mourned by his widow and young children. As the newspaper account is read out they fall silent; and in this ominous silence we hear the first strains of the theme that gives the novel its title: "Cry for the broken tribe, for the law and custom that is gone. . . . Cry, the beloved country that those things are not yet at an end" (74). Kumalo's premonition that the missing Absalom might be involved in the crime weighs him down. He tells Msimangu there is nothing in his heart but fear.

Kumalo's intense sense of fear is immediately universalized in a chorus of white voices comprising the greater part of chapter 12, where the focus of interest shifts from the old clergyman's personal experience of fear to the more general sensation of fear that pervades the land—the beloved country—as a consequence of racial tensions. In the course of this episode, commencing with the refrain line, "Have no doubt there is fear in the land," various constituencies within white South African society grapple with the question of what is to be done in the face of all-pervading fear.

Technically, this episode is a remarkable achievement; and, in some respects, its dramatic method resembles that of T. S. Eliot's *The Waste Land*. In that poem Eliot achieved extraordinary compression for his major theme of moral breakdown and loss of vitality in modern urban society. He did this primarily by arranging his epic work not in narrative sequence but in short, contrasting, emotionally charged dramatic fragments spoken by a variety of voices. As a consequence of this technique, the varying and contrasting voices in *The Waste Land* have a cumulative "stereophonic" effect far more powerful than that of a single narrative voice.

In *Cry, the Beloved Country* Paton employs a similar dramatic method to embody the vague sense of fear and futility that paralyzes the will of white South African society. He develops a series of dramatic "frames" set off in the text by rows of asterisks, in which contending voices cry out about what must be done. Most of the brief vignettes in this sequence take the form of moments of contention between opposing views. But the elements in this sequence are not mere fragments that could be rearranged in some other order. They follow a purposeful progression leading to a point of hopeless impasse between optimism and despair—a climactic point appropriate for the repetition of the phrase that provides the novel's title, first raised to fill the ominous silence in the clergy house following the news of the death of Arthur Jarvis. But in this instance it is followed by a significant variation warning against a love that is too deep: "Cry, the beloved country, for the unborn child that is the inheritor of our fear. Let him not love the earth too deeply" (80).

A close reading of this sequence of dramatic vignettes will reveal a progressive accumulation of emotional intensity leading up to this significant variation. Following the brief prelude on fear and the hundred voices crying out about what must be done, individual voices address town gatherings. The first speaker demands more police protection and is applauded. The second speaker, sounding like

Paton's articles on crime prevention in the *Forum*, responds that, except temporarily, more police cannot be the answer; people must first have worthy purposes and worthy goals to work for. The fact that both speakers are applauded shows that the hearers also are hopelessly divided and uncertain.

The three segments that follow are composed primarily of dialogue representing opposing views. The first of these retains some of the formality of the town meeting with which the sequence began; but as the contending speakers assail each other alternately, the quality of the discussion deteriorates from the quasiformal to the banal. The subject is black education. The first speaker, who follows the polite formality of addressing the chairman, supports the need for more education. The opposing speaker, who feels blacks are being spoiled by too much education, is sharply sarcastic (as Dr. Verwoerd, the architect of apartheid, had been in his attacks on Paton). This speaker ignores the chairman and launches into a racist monologue.

Next, a pair of voices offer opposing views on the benefits of enforcing "the Pass Laws"—a complex set of laws for controlling the movement of black persons in white areas. Since each speaker is set in his views their "talking" about the problem is aimless.

The third pair of voices are those of two society women from the suburban tennis club set. These women are pitifully class-conscious. (Their children have English "society" names like Penelope.) Typical of their class, they see themselves as sympathetic toward the problems of black servants, but, characteristically, they do not want places of recreation for those servants in their neighborhoods.

At this point the nature of the sequence of segments changes again, and the separate contending voices of dialogue meld into a generalized voice speaking from a level above the hubbub of the hundred voices crying. The initial segment of this part of the sequence has two paragraphs. In the first of these the views for and against apartheid are represented indirectly: "And some cry for the cutting up of South Africa without delay into separate areas. . . . And others cry away with the compound system . . . and they ask for the establishment of villages for the laborers in the mines" (78). (The compound system, long used in the Johannesburg gold mines, brought men from rural and tribal areas to the mines for extended periods as indentured laborers. They lived in "compounds," or single men's dormitories, away from their wives and children.)

The contrasting voices that continue the topic in the second paragraph of this segment are, in South African terms, those of "the English-speaking churches" and "the Afrikaans-speaking churches." The former—chiefly Anglican, Roman Catholic, Methodist, Baptist, and Congregational—cry for more education and opportunity. The latter stand firm on the traditional policy of no equality in church or state, and they support the prime objective of apartheid that required "the native people" to develop along their own lines.

In the course of the next two segments the opposing views meld increasingly into a single voice in which the emotional force grows steadily more powerful. The voice declares that besides getting more locks for the doors, people will get fierce dogs and look to their own security. And just as the opposing arguments in the earlier sequences of dialogue led nowhere, so the prophetic voice in this sequence concludes that there will be no action: people will live from day to day and not think about the fundamental problem at all.

From this vision of a vague, fearful future and of the paralysis of the will, the action is brought back sharply to the present by a shift in tone to the crisp businesslike rhythms of a voice announcing that there will be meetings in Parkwold and elsewhere tonight on the subject of crime. But at one meeting, that of the Cathedral Guild, there will be gloom. For the speaker of the evening, Arthur Jarvis, has been shot dead. At this point—the emotional culmination of the series of dramatic frames on the divided mind of white South Africa—the prophetic voice repeats, with significant variation, the phrases that provide the novel's title: "Cry, the beloved country, for the unborn child that is the inheritor of our fear. Let him not love the earth too deeply" (80).

In the enigmatic phrases that follow this repetition of the title phrase—"Let him not laugh too gladly . . . nor give too much of his heart to mountain and valley"—the prophetic voice implies that a certain kind of romantic love of country can be excessive and destructive. This is what the poet W. B. Yeats also implies in lines on the single-minded devotion of the Irish patriotic rebels in the poem "Easter, 1916": "And what if excess of love / Bewildered them till they died?"

At this moment of heightened tension, with the prophetic voice warning against too much love of country, the scene shifts back, without break or transition, to Kumalo's mounting fears. Mrs. Ndlela of End Street comes to tell Msimangu that the police have been to her home looking for Absalom and that she told them he had moved on to Mrs. Mkize's in Alexandra. Fearful that Absalom is wanted on some serious matter, Kumalo and Msimangu pursue a series of leads that brings them back to Alexandra, to Shanty Town, to the reformatory, and to the girl's place in Pimville, only to find out at each place that the police have been there before them.

The mounting tension of this episode is then relieved by what, on the surface, appears to be a quiet interlude: the visit to Ezenzeleni where the blind are rehabilitated. But it is only the frenzied physical activity that has been eased. Kumalo's inner turmoil continues and brings him to the verge of despair. While Msimangu attends to his affairs at Ezenzeleni, Kumalo finds a solitary place where he reflects on the fate of Absalom and others like him and on the broken tribe that cannot be mended. When Msimangu comes to bring him to lunch, he finds Kumalo so dispirited that he is compelled to warn him of the dangers of despair and loss of faith: "This is madness . . . it is also a sin . . . I speak to you as a priest" (89).

The themes of hope and despair are major themes in *Cry, the Beloved Country*, and in any appraisal of them, particularly as they are made manifest in the main character, this interlude at Ezenzeleni assumes a place of importance equaling, for example, that of the choral scenes in discussions of the public political themes.

On the day after the visit to Ezenzeleni, while Kumalo is dealing with Gertrude's affairs, Msimangu and the young man from the reformatory arrive to tell him what he has feared: Absalom has been arrested for the Parkwold murder, along with two accomplices: Johannes Pafuri and Matthew Kumalo, son of the priest's brother, John. Kumalo goes first to inform his brother of the bad news, and together they accompany Msimangu and the social worker to the prison where Kumalo visits Absalom and John visits Matthew.

The situation in which Stephen Kumalo finally finds his lost son is distressing for both. The painful scene between them is dramatically effective—partly, no doubt, because Paton is able to draw on his long professional experience in dealing with delinquent youths, and partly because of his interest in the theme of difficult relationships between fathers and sons. This is the principal theme of his second novel, *Too Late the Phalarope,* which may have derived some of its elements from his having experienced a difficult relationship with his own father, a violent and authoritarian man, "who lived by a narrow morality; insisted on obedience in trivial things; used physical punishment on his sons, and very likely, at times, on his wife."[1]

In the prison scene Absalom is frightened and helpless. He cannot find reasons for his behavior; but he confesses to the murder and agrees to go forward with his planned marriage to the pregnant girl if it can be arranged. After leaving Absalom, Kumalo and the others join John Kumalo who seizes on the news that Absalom has admitted to the murder before witnesses. John declares that he will employ a lawyer to represent his son separately, because, apart from Absalom's word, there is no proof that his son and Johannes Pafuri were at the murder scene. "Who will believe your son?" he asks his brother, cruelly; and Kumalo, who has been brought near to despair, seeks help from Father Vincent. This theme of despair, like the contrasting one of hope, is a fundamental theme in *Cry, the Beloved Country.* It also has particular significance in the characterization of Stephen Kumalo.

The shadow of loss clouds Stephen Kumalo's life from the novel's opening scenes: his son, his sister, and his brother have gone away and are no longer heard from. But he never wholly abandons hope. For example, until the need arises to use it for the journey to Johannesburg, he keeps the money saved to send Absalom to St. Chad's school, in the hope that it may still be used for its original purpose. The initial stages of his search in Johannesburg find him almost constantly in a state of anxiety in which hope and fear contend; but after he hears of the murder of Arthur Jarvis his fear begins to lead him to the threshold of despair, which, as both Msimangu and Father Vincent have occasion to remind him, is a serious matter for a Christian priest.

The first indications of Kumalo's temptation to despair become evident immediately following the reading of the newspaper account of the murder in Parkwold. As the two priests leave the rectory and Kumalo is full of foreboding, Msimangu suggests that they pray together. But Kumalo, whose habit in times of stress has always been to resort to prayer, declines the invitation, saying that there is no prayer left in him. A few days later, after he hears that the police are seeking Absalom, he tells Msimangu that he has found nothing during his solitary meditation but more fear and pain. He adds, in a bitter declaration of despair that shocks Msimangu: "There is nothing in the world but fear and pain" (89).

The third and most dramatic occasion in which the theme of Kumalo's temptation to despair arises is the scene with Father Vincent following the discovery that Absalom is a confessed murderer and that there is need for a lawyer for his defense. Some of the matter of this scene has reverberations that carry over to the novel's closing scene; and it is also the scene that has the closest bearing on the novel's subtitle: "A Story of Comfort in Desolation." Additionally, it has obvious bearing on the symbolic significance of Kumalo's Christian name, that of the martyr, Saint Stephen.

Kumalo begins this scene in which Father Vincent senses his temptation to despair with a recapitulation of the stages of his search. He tells of the steady growth of his anxiety and fear until, on hearing of the murder, the feelings grew into something "too great to be borne." He speaks, too, of his and his wife's lack of foreknowledge of his son's evil ways. This leads him into his striking parable of the man sleeping in the grass who is unaware of his coming destruction.

Father Vincent seeks to console him by saying that the fear and anxiety led to sorrow, which is at least an arriving—an idea he, too, expresses in the symbolic language that is "like the Zulu tongue." But Kumalo will not be easily comforted. Once again he directly utters despairing words when he replies that it seems God has turned from him. It is then that Father Vincent, as Msimangu had done before him, tells Kumalo that he must speak to him as a priest. He urges Kumalo not to seek to understand the secret ways of God; and he repeatedly uses the word *secret* to signify the will of God. He says that the answer to what life is, is a secret; that what urges Kumalo to compassion for the girl is a secret; that why one goes on when it might seem better to die is a secret. And he makes clear that Kumalo, the priest and man of God, must accept the secret will of God. That Kumalo profits from this counsel is evident in the intentional echoes of this scene in the book's final passages. As the sun rises over the beloved country on the morning of Absalom's execution the prophetic voice of the narrator says: "But when the dawn will come from the fear of bondage and the bondage of fear, why, that is a secret" (277).

The English theologian, Professor Horton Davies, finds that the portrait of Father Vincent in this scene in *Cry, the Beloved Country,* although brief, mirrors the essential qualities of a priest and confessor. First, Davies says, "like all confessors he is an excellent listener . . . He knows when a man has become so dumb with grief that no words can comfort him." Second, as a "surgeon of the soul" he can speak severely, even in such circumstances, to recall Kumalo to his vocation as a priest. And third, he is a practical man who counsels Kumalo to pray "in a severely practical way" for Gertrude, and for the girl, and for all at the Mission House and Ezenzeleni who try to rebuild in a place of destruction.

In summary, book 1 of *Cry, the Beloved Country* chronicles Kumalo's successive hopes and disappointments in his search for his son, Absalom. The account of how Kumalo's premonitions lead to paralyzing fear is sustained above the level of conventional melodrama, in part by Paton's skilled use of artistic devices, and in part by the qualities of those representatives of hope who lend Kumalo support: his grave and thoughtful guide, Msimangu; Father Vincent and the other priests at the clergy house; and the workers at the reform school. Book 1 ends with Kumalo going about the practical business of doing what he can for Absalom; arranging for his defense and for his marriage; and bringing the girl who will be his daughter-in-law to join Gertrude and her son at Mrs. Lithebe's in the restored family.

chapter 8

Arthur Jarvis:
A Vision of Hope

Book 2 of *Cry, the Beloved Country* begins with a repetition of the first part of the lyric passage about the lovely road that runs from Ixopo into the rich green hills that opened book 1. But here the lyric does not take the counterturn from the high valleys of white farms where the grass is green and matted to the contrasting red eroded soil about Ndotsheni in the African reserve below. For in book 2 we leave the primarily black world of Stephen Kumalo and his son, Absalom, and enter the primarily white world of James Jarvis and his son, Arthur. We do this at first chiefly through the stream of consciousness in the mind of James Jarvis who owns High Place, one of the finest farms in the countryside.

It is October and time for spring plowing in that land south of the equator; but the drought has made the soil of the flat plowed fields iron-hard, and Jarvis walks with his dog to the hilltop to look for signs of rain. As he climbs he sees the red bare hills of the black reservation below, and he thinks of how white farmers like himself have begun to fear that the desolation of erosion might spread to their farms also. It is at the point where Jarvis's thoughts begin to be occupied with this problem that Paton creates for us the mind of a typical white farmer of the English-speaking community of Natal of that period—all the more typical because Jarvis is thinking of the frequently expressed views of his fellow white farmers. Their perspective on the land of the neighboring African reserve, and of the black community trying to scratch a living from it, is remarkable for its sense of apartness and almost complete detachment. For example, it passes through Jarvis's mind that each year less food is grown in "these reserves"; and that "these people" don't know how to plow along the contours or build walls to save the soil. Expressions like "these reserves" and "these people" imply a typical segregationist attitude to a people looked upon as different—a people apart, for whom one feels no direct sense of responsibility.

While he muses on the problem of the overcrowded reserves, badly eroded through overgrazing and inexpert plowing, Jarvis's mind turns to endless discussions with his fellow farmers of what might be done—endless because these discussions, like those of the chorus of city voices in book 1, simply go around and around in circles without practical consequences. Typical arguments put forward by various neighboring farmers come into his mind. Some say there should be more education; others say the educated would leave the land. Some say there should be more land; but others, who object to this, want to know where such land will come from and who will work for the white farmers; and so on, without conclusion. Turning these thoughts over in his mind, Jarvis looks about on the rich green hills he inherited from his father. He had hoped that his only son would inherit the land from him, but his son chose to be an engineer rather than a farmer and went away to Johannesburg, where he now lives with his wife and children.

At this juncture Jarvis observes a police car approaching his house down below. He assumes it is the local white Afrikaans-speaking constable, Binnendyk, on patrol; and his musings turn to the growing number of Afrikaners in government employment—in the police department and the civil service—in English-speaking Natal, where there were none in his father's day. And as Jarvis is conscious of himself as someone apart from the tribal people in the reserves, so also he is conscious of himself as a person apart from the white Afrikaners, separated not on the basis of race but on historical grounds. An earlier generation of English-speakers and Afrikaans-speakers had fought the bitter Boer War on Natal battlefields just over forty years before: "His own father had sworn he would disinherit any child of his who married an Afrikaner, but times had changed" (132). The arrival of the police on the hillside brings Jarvis's musing to an end. They have tragic news. His son, Arthur, has been shot to death by an intruder in his home in Parkwold, Johannesburg, just hours before. Now he must tell his wife and prepare to go to Johannesburg.

On arriving in Johannesburg Jarvis and his wife stay with his son's wife's parents, the Harrisons. The elder Harrison, a businessman employed by the gold mines, has strong reservations about the views of his murdered son-in-law, Arthur Jarvis. Oblivious to the element of blackmail in it, he even admits that he passed on a warning to the young man to be more discreet in his attacks on the Chamber of Mines for their treatment of African laborers, or he would risk the loss of mine business by the company that employed him. Harrison's son, John, however, is an ardent admirer of Arthur Jarvis's liberal views; and it is through him that James Jarvis becomes acquainted with some of his son's social projects such as the Claremont African Boys' Club.

Jarvis learns from his hosts of messages of condolence "from the Bishop, and the Acting Prime Minister, and the Mayor"; from organizations like the Daughters of Africa; and from "coloured people" and Indians and Jews. From the items on this list it seems that Paton put much from his own experience into the characterization of Arthur Jarvis. The messages from people of various races and faiths, and their later presence at the funeral, recall Paton's "deep experience" at the funeral of Mrs. Edith Jones, the white woman from Johannesburg who (as detailed in chapter 2, above) received similar tributes. The passage of time since Paton wrote the novel has brought even greater significance to the mention of messages from "the Bishop and the Acting Prime Minister," because, in 1946, these dignitaries were the Anglican bishop, Geoffrey Clayton, and Paton's friend, Jan Hofmeyr, both of whose lives Paton was later to write in his *Apartheid and the Arch-bishop* and his *Hofmeyr* (published, slightly abridged, in the United States as *South African Tragedy*). The prevailing theme in both of these writings, as in the development of the character of Arthur Jarvis, is emancipation of a white South African from conventional prejudices.

The elder Harrison tells James Jarvis that his son, Arthur, learned to speak Afrikaans—and reveals his own jingoistic prejudices by adding, "It's a lingo I know nothing about, thank God" (139). Harrison also informs Jarvis that his son spoke Zulu, and that to learn Afrikaans he had spent time on an Afrikaner farm. Paton himself, who also spoke Zulu and had stayed on an Afrikaner farm while learning Afrikaans, is clearly the model for this aspect of the character of Arthur Jarvis; and, as his writings for the *Forum* bear out, he also incorporated other parts of his own experience in the life of the younger Jarvis who, according to Harrison, was "always speaking here and there" of "Native crime and Native schools" and that "kind of thing" (139).

The murdered man, Arthur Jarvis, never comes on stage before us in the novel. He is nevertheless the character about whom we learn the most. The reader comes to know Arthur Jarvis, as his father, James Jarvis, belatedly comes to know him: through his letters and writings; through the many books in his study; and even through his choice of pictures to hang on its walls. One reason why the comparatively brief portrait of Arthur Jarvis in *Cry, the Beloved Country* seems so complete and so effectively drawn is that the materials supplied us from his life and works are similar to the materials on which a good biography is ordinarily based. Another reason for the effectiveness of the portrait is that the character of Arthur Jarvis represents an ideal in which Paton was passionately interested.

James Jarvis's first introduction to the quality of his son's mind comes from the letters on the dead man's desk—the invitations to speak, for example, at the Claremont African Boys' Club, of which he was president—and from the several writings on social justice his son left behind. These writings argue the case for racial conciliation in South Africa from the Christian and liberal standpoint that Paton shared with Jan Hofmeyr. They begin to open James Jarvis's eyes to the real plight of both urban and rural Africans as a consequence of the destruction of their tribal organization without provision for its replacement by something better.

The manuscript Arthur Jarvis was writing at the time of his death, and which his father reads after the funeral, is also on the theme of moral responsibility. But in this instance (since his audience was to be the Cathedral Guild) there is an emphasis on Christian responsibility in a country where the term "Christian civilization" was adopted as a self-description by much of the white community. Before breaking off at the phrase, "Allow me a minute," interrupted by the murderer, it concludes: "The truth is that our civilization is not Christian, it is a tragic compound of great ideal and fearful practice . . . of loving charity and fearful clutching of possessions" (155). The theologian Horton Davies finds this diagnosis to be "subtle as well as profound, in its exploration of the dilemmas in South Africa and the utter contradictions."[1]

The key to the significance of the character of Arthur Jarvis is provided in chapter 24 in the "Private essay on the Evolution of a South African" discovered in his desk drawer by his father. This essay begins with a passage on the vexing questions concerning the national identity of people of varied racial backgrounds living in South Africa: "Who is a South African?" and "How does one become a South African?" In considering these questions Arthur Jarvis writes: "It is hard to be born a South African. One can be born an Afrikaner, or an English-speaking South African, or a coloured man, or a Zulu. . . . One can see, as I saw when I was a boy, the reserves of the Bantu people and see nothing that was happening there at all" (174). Reading this essay in his son's study, James Jarvis finds that his murdered son, Arthur, had sought to become something new: a South African who strove to rise above the old antagonisms and above discrimination on the basis of race or language and to become a nonracial South African—an ideal to which Alan Paton himself was subsequently to devote a great part of his life in the Liberal Party.

If every picture tells a story, Arthur Jarvis's choice of pictures for the walls of his study provides a good indication of what the man most valued as emotionally significant. There are four of them: "Christ crucified, and Abraham Lincoln, and the white gabled house of Vergelegen, and a painting of leafless willows by a river in a wintery veld" (143). The first of these pictures represents what Jarvis valued most: his Christian faith. The second shows his admiration for the man he recognized as the world's greatest champion of racial justice—who was not a South African. The third, a picture of a historic architectural gem, is the house Simon van der Stel had built after his arrival in 1662 to administer the Dutch East India Company's settlement at the Cape of Good Hope, and from which an architecture recognizably South African was derived. This house at Vergelegen would be as readily recognizable by a South African as part of the country's architectural heritage as, let us say, Thomas Jefferson's Monticello, or even the White House, would be recognized by Americans as part of their heritage.

The fourth picture, the "painting of leafless willows by a river in a wintery veld," symbolizes Jarvis's love of the land itself even in the most bleak and desolate of the seasons; for as the prairies symbolize the native land to North Americans, and the pampas to South Americans, so the veld speaks of home to South Africans. Of course Paton does not interpret the pictures for us in this way. As is the case with any pictures, we must bring something to them. From personal acquaintance with Paton I know that he was extraordinarily alert to details and nuances in literature and art—and indeed to the details of natural scenes wherever he visited. He always wanted to know the names of local flowers and trees and birds. In the light of this knowledge, I shall venture a reconsideration of the one picture of the four that has no obvious associations, the winter scene in the veld, as if we were seeing it through his eyes.

The person who would treasure such a scene is not a newly arrived colonist from somewhere else or a "transplanted" Englishman (as some English-speaking South Africans like Harrison, and of course the early settlers, regarded themselves). In 1969 I went with Paton to an exhibition of historical paintings at Rhodes University, Grahamstown, commemorating the English settlers of the 1820s in South Af-

rica. The pictures were mainly paintings of farm and settlement scenes
with buildings and wagons and so forth, and I noticed nothing in them
beyond that until Paton drew my attention to details of flowers
painted into some foregrounds. These were, as he said, typical English
wildflowers that did not grow in South Africa. What these settlers had
painted were familiar flowers from a remembered English or Scottish
landscape. These newcomers had not yet grown to know, or to love,
the native flowers of the veld. They were not at heart South Africans,
but transplanted Englishmen—as the early New Englanders also considered themselves to be. As his choice of paintings demonstrate, Arthur Jarvis had become a South African—but in a way even his father
found it difficult to comprehend.

Just as interpretation of Jarvis's choice of pictures requires some
thought on the reader's part, so does understanding some of the other
things the murdered man has left behind. The many books in the
Afrikaans language, for example, reveal a mentality quite different
from that of the elder Harrison, who could say, "It's a lingo I know
nothing about, thank God." And it is quite evident, too, that we must
bring some knowledge of Abraham Lincoln to the young man's writings; otherwise, we will fail to fully understand them. James Jarvis, a
man of little reading, is astonished to find in his son's study a whole
bookcase full of books about Lincoln. Browsing in these, he reads
Lincoln's Gettysburg Address and, later, his Second Inaugural Address. Some of the father's subsequent actions are motivated by what
he encounters in Lincoln's writings—something readers of *Cry, the
Beloved Country* who do not carry Lincoln's words at Gettysburg and
in the Second Inaugural in their memories may overlook, for Paton
does not supply the relevant passages.

In particular, he does not supply the passage from the Gettysburg
Address that apparently guides the father in deciding what form a suit-
able memorial to his son might take: "It is rather for us to be here
dedicated to the great task remaining before us—that from these hon-
ored dead we take increased devotion to the cause for which they gave
the last full measure of devotion; that we here highly resolve that these
dead shall not have died in vain." Neither does Paton supply a passage

from Lincoln's Second Inaugural Address that might equally have influenced Jarvis's choice of memorial; that is, the fervent plea for restoration with which the Second Inaugural Address closes: "to bind up the nation's wounds; to care for him who shall have borne the battle, and for his widow, and his orphan—to do all which may achieve and cherish a just and lasting peace among ourselves, and with all nations."[2]

It is difficult to know why Paton, while revealing in the novel that Jarvis slipped the volume of Lincoln in his pocket for further reading, did not choose to provide his readers with the pertinent passages. Had he done so, not only would the elder Jarvis's motives be more readily recognized, but much of the adverse criticism of book 3 on the grounds of Jarvis's actions might have been anticipated. It seems possible that Paton assumed that most readers would have such passages in their memory as he had. He undoubtedly knew by heart many passages in prose and verse including Walt Whitman's elegy for Lincoln, "When Lilacs Last in the Door-yard Bloom'd." In *For You Departed,* a memorial for his first wife, Paton quotes the opening lines of this elegy: "When lilacs last in the door-yard bloom'd, / And the great star early droop'd in the western sky in the night, / I mourn'd, and yet shall mourn with ever-returning spring."[3] I once heard him turn aside from his text at a public reading of passages from *For You Departed* to say how much he admired Whitman's "great threnody," as he called it, and to encourage everyone to learn it and teach it; after which he recited from memory the continuation of the opening lines: "Ever-returning spring, trinity sure to me you bring, / Lilac blooming perennial and drooping star in the west, / And thought of him I love." In the last piece of writing of his life, an unfinished essay for *Time,* Paton again quoted these six lines, calling them "one of the most memorable tributes paid by any human being to another."[4]

Paton's admiration for Lincoln appears to have been a long-standing thing, not merely a temporary enthusiasm. While attending a conference on penal reform in Washington, D.C., in November 1946, he wrote the chapters in his novel in which the character of Arthur Jarvis is developed. He recalled that in the course of this visit the Lincoln Memorial impressed him as "a temple erected to the spirit of man at its highest and purest"; and that he mounted its steps "with a feeling akin to awe, and stood for a long time before the seated figure of one of the greatest men of history, surely the greatest of all the rulers of nations, the man who would spend a sleepless night because he had been asked to order the execution of a young soldier. He certainly knew that in pardoning we are pardoned."[5]

James Jarvis's discovery of how far his son had ventured into deep waters following a set of ideals that included the spirit of Lincoln occupies parts of several chapters in *Cry, the Beloved Country* leading up to the trial of Absalom Kumalo. The trial scene opens, in a language of solemn formality, with a description of the setting for the trial in a segregated South African courtroom. This description develops into a commentary on the majesty of the law, the status of judges, and the significance of court ceremonial. The commentary includes an indirect attack on unjust laws and the dilemma of judges who must administer them: "The Judge does not make the Law. It is the People that make the Law. Therefore if the Law is unjust, and if the Judge judges according to the Law, that is justice, even if it is not just" (158).

The unjust laws that Paton has in mind in this passage, although not mentioned specifically, are probably the hated "Pass Laws" of that period that applied only to Africans, who were required to carry at all times various identification documents known as "passes" under penalty of fine or imprisonment. Ironically, the dilemma of just judges was to increase dramatically on this score in South Africa soon after the publication of *Cry, the Beloved Country.*

The framework of apartheid erected by Afrikaner Nationalists after 1948 consisted of many complex laws separating people on the basis of race—black, white, Indian, and mixed race—in every conceivable area of life: in places of residence; in education; in trains and on buses; in exits and entrances; in sports, in cinemas, and on park benches; in church services including the marriage service.

Particularly during the decade of the sixties, the many laws establishing apartheid were reinforced by a second series of punitive laws that applied only to those who disagreed with apartheid and opposed it or protested against it. Under these harsh laws, which greatly intensified the dilemma of judges, the authorities were given vast powers of punishment outside the courts and legal system. These powers included detention without trial, house arrest, and banning. Many of these powers, over which the courts had no authority, were first introduced during the state of emergency imposed by the government following the Sharpeville massacre in 1960 when the police fired into an African crowd. In the climate created by these new laws, Paton's passages on the law in this episode of *Cry, the Beloved Country* no doubt acquired greater resonance.

At the trial, Absalom makes a poor witness on his own behalf; and the prosecutor has little difficulty in supporting his case for a verdict of premeditated murder. Absalom's defense collapses in the face of the strategy devised by his uncle, John Kumalo, when his cousin, Matthew, and Johannes Pafuri deny their presence at the scene.

chapter 9

James Jarvis:
Emancipation

In *Cry, the Beloved Country* the interval between the court's adjournment after Absalom's trial and its reconvening for his sentencing is occupied by five brief chapters, each of great interest. In the first of these chapters the scope of the concern for justice widens out from the particular case of Absalom's trial to the more general problem of social justice in South Africa. The occasion for opening up this new perspective is the account of the discovery of new, rich gold deposits at Odendaalsrust in the Orange Free State. This account is based on an actual event in South Africa at the time of the novel's setting that had, in fact, sent the Johannesburg stock exchange into frenzied activity.

In chapter 23 Paton satirizes the monied and mining interests, chiefly English-speaking, that built Johannesburg as a commercial center largely through the exploitation of cheap labor, and, in particular, through the "compound system" that brought many thousands of black laborers to the mines from distant places without provision for wives and children to accompany them. The sole representative of the commercial class with mining interests we have met up to this point in the novel is Mr. Harrison, father-in-law of the murdered man, Arthur Jarvis. We know that Harrison defends the compound system, that he argued with his son-in-law about it, and even brought him a warning from the Chamber of Mines, accompanied by a veiled threat, not to go too far in opposing the system.

In the broader perspective of this chapter, Paton's satire is laced with some bitter humor. He depicts the mining interests, and the English-speaking community in general, not only as being segregationist-minded and exploitive of blacks but also as despising their Afrikaans-speaking fellow whites whose language they disdain as unpronounceable. One form his satire takes is to show these jingoists as slaves to hackneyed thinking. They speak in clichés: "A new lease of life, they say, South Africa is to have a new lease of life."

Occasionally the humor is too local in its implications to be readily apparent now; as, for example, in the case of the imaginary speaker who feels that the unpronounceable Afrikaans names should be changed to something easier like Smuts and Hofmeyr. But the speaker has second thoughts about Hofmeyr; not really for the ostensible reason that there is already a place of that name, but apparently because of his unspoken realization that a reminder of the liberal-minded Deputy Prime Minister, Jan Hofmeyr, would not be welcomed by the conservative Chamber of Mines. Since Hofmeyr, who was Paton's friend, is not a developed character in the novel, most readers are unlikely to respond to such private humor.

On the other hand, some parts of the satire—particularly the whole central section on the value of stock market profits—may seem even more timely now, following the debates during the Reagan years in the United States, and the Thatcher era in Britain, over what was satirically called "the trickle-down" theory of economics that some have summarized in the humorous aphorism: "When the rich have more spending money, the poor will benefit." But Paton's satire, however humorous, never devolves into mere vituperation; and we are never allowed to lose sight of the fact that there is a real human problem at issue. He provides for the opposing views of the humanitarian-minded, and he makes an exception in the case of the mining magnate, Sir Ernest Oppenheimer, who had proposed replacing the compound system with villages where workers could live with their families.

In his article, "The 'Message' of Alan Paton," F. Charles Rooney describes this chapter as an excellent example of Paton's technique of "expressing the innermost emotions of a whole nation" independently of any particular character in the story. Rooney says that while this chapter may seem, at first, to be an interpolation by the author as narrator, it is, in fact, "a natural and integral part of his story, a sequel to the brilliant ninth chapter which describes the overnight rise of a shanty village." Rooney views the chapter as "a stinging rebuke to the gold fever of the rich white men who own the mines and unmercifully exploit native labor"; and he adds that to deny a legitimate place in literature to the kind of judgment the chapter expresses, "is surely to take such an exclusive and rarefied view of the writing art that it no longer touches life."[1]

Rooney's assessment supports the view that the several chapters of seeming interpolation in *Cry, the Beloved Country*—principally, chapters 6, 9, and 23—have the valid purpose of widening the novel's perspective to include South Africa as a whole. It was, no doubt, on the basis of these chapters that Maxwell Perkins formed the opinion that South Africa, itself, is a character in the novel. One might add that the placement of chapter 23 is also purposeful on another count. It bears a subtle relationship to the chapter that follows on James Jarvis's deep experience among the books and papers in his son's study.

The satirical picture of the white Johannesburg commercial class in the first chapter following Absalom's trial provides a contrasting background for the crucial private moment in the life of James Jarvis when he revisits his son's study. In a general sense Jarvis comes from the same English-speaking class as Harrison and the Johannesburg commercial community. When he first comes to Johannesburg he listens to Harrison's conservative views without objection; and he admits to puzzlement at the path his son has taken. But his first two visits to his son's study began to prepare him to set his foot on a path out from that mental environment. In the course of chapter 24 we see a further stage in his emancipation from the conventional assumptions of his class and generation.

Because of Paton's method of quiet understatement, we do not see this moment dramatically; nor are we directly told that a change has occurred. We are left on our own to discern the awakening of Jarvis's conscience as, with him, we read his son's "Private Essay on the Evolution of a South African." The opening passages of this essay outline the view that it is possible to grow up, as Arthur Jarvis did, in a good, tolerant, white family in South Africa and yet remain ignorant of the true situation of blacks in that country. His father is shocked and hurt when he reads this. In his agitation he leaves the study and goes downstairs to the passage still stained with his son's blood. But on second thought he returns to the study and continues reading the remainder of the essay. There he encounters his son's eloquent declaration of intention to do what is right, not what is expedient or in conformity with public opinion.

Jarvis then sits a long time in thought before coming to a decision. We are not told what he thinks or decides; only that he takes his hat and leaves the house, not by way of the bloodstained passage but through the front door. The policeman on duty interprets this as a sign that Jarvis is unable to face the bloodstain again; but he is mistaken. Ironically, the significance of Jarvis's taking a new route is that he has decided on a new departure. He has determined to put behind him his sorrowing over his son's murder and to take up his son's cause with the consequent change in his own life and attitudes. Since this is an inner spiritual change, we do not observe it externally. We are left to infer it, and the new decisiveness in the man's movements supports our inference.

Chapter 25, the third chapter, filling the interval between Absalom's trial and his sentencing, may be the finest chapter in *Cry, the Beloved Country* as a literary accomplishment. As Edmund Fuller says: "There is no finer scene in a consistently moving book than that in which Stephen Kumalo and James Jarvis first come face to face by chance . . . and realize one another's identities."[2] This chapter bears rereading both for its representation of deeply felt emotion and for its effective handling of the dramatic devices that give the scene much of its power.

On one of the days when the court is not in session, James Jarvis and his wife visit her favorite niece, Barbara Smith from Ixopo, now married and living in the town of Springs, near Johannesburg. The two women decide to go into the town and they leave Jarvis reading the newspaper with its account of the discovery of gold and the rapid rise of stock prices. Answering a knock on the back door, Jarvis finds an old African clergyman at the foot of the kitchen steps who appears to him to be fearful, trembling, and greatly distressed.

What then ensues is a classic instance of what Aristotle calls a "recognition scene" in tragic drama. We, as readers, know what James Jarvis does not know: namely, that the trembling old man is the Reverent Stephen Kumalo from Ndotsheni, near his own farm, High Place, and that Kumalo's son has murdered Jarvis's son. The reader of the novel will, no doubt, recall that the friend who helped Kumalo carry his bag on the morning he left Ndotsheni by train had asked a favor of him regarding "Sibeko's daughter." Sibeko's daughter had worked for the daughter of a man named Smith in Ixopo and had accompanied her to Springs after her marriage. But Sibeko had not heard from his daughter in a long time, and the favor asked of Kumalo was that while in Johannesburg he should try to trace her. It is this mission of mercy that brings Kumalo to the house in Springs while James Jarvis is visiting there. The reader's possession of this knowledge, of which one of the characters in the scene is ignorant, constitutes dramatic irony; and, as always, it intensifies interest.

This encounter between the two fathers is essential to the plot of *Cry, the Beloved Country*. The reader is prepared for it by the talk of Sibeko's daughter in an early episode; and much of the subsequent outcome in book 3 arises from this encounter. Like many such recognition scenes in literature, it is open to objection on the grounds of unlikely coincidence; however, the simultaneous arrival of Oedipus and his unknown father at the crossroads where three roads meet is an even more unlikely coincidence. In relation to dramatic works, such objections have little relevance. As we watch events unfolding before us on the stage, we are engaged by the *dramatic* truth of events and involved in them by what Coleridge calls "a willing suspension of disbelief." How effectively we are drawn into this situation depends on the skill of the writer. In his play *Oedipus the King*, Sophocles holds audiences spellbound as Oedipus discovers a succession of horrors including marriage with his mother. Sophocles succeeds in this primarily through the device of dramatic irony: the audiences at his play know the things of which Oedipus is ignorant. So also in this scene in Paton's novel the readers know the identity of the old man of which Jarvis is ignorant.

Another dramatic device, whereby skilled writers prepare an audience to accept outcomes they might otherwise question, is the rapidity of the dramatic action itself. Shakespeare's *Othello* is a classic example of this. A critic might say that if Othello stopped to think, even for a moment, he would see through Iago's scheme. But Shakespeare doesn't allow either Othello or the audience time to think. In *Othello* alone, of all Shakespeare's great tragedies, there is no lull in act 4, before the tragic climax of act 5. Instead, the action accelerates rapidly through successive crises while audience interest grows more intense. As his material at the start of this chapter demands, Paton employs a corresponding device of rapid unfolding of events. The immediate preliminaries to the meeting of the two fathers—the account of the visit to Springs, Jarvis's walk in the garden, the conversation of the women, their decision to go to town, his reading of the newspaper accounts of new gold discoveries, and so on—are told with extraordinary economy in two brief paragraphs, through which the reader is carried along at a rapid pace up to the crucial moment: "While he was reading there was a knock at the kitchen door, and he went out to find a native parson standing on the paved stone" (177).

This chapter is also worth notice for the effective handling of the dialogue between the two fathers and for the details of other dramatic elements employed. It is easy to imagine this recognition scene staged in a theater; and a good test of dramatic effectiveness is to envision how actors might interpret each role. If one puts the scene to that test, it may soon become apparent that Paton, who wrote plays as a young man, may very well have done this himself in the writing of the chapter. For example, Kumalo's actions of sitting with his head bowed, of dropping the stick and hat, of struggling to rise, and of dropping the papers from his trembling hands, are actions an actor might have thought up to interpret a character in just such an emotional situation. So are Jarvis's hesitant movements in picking up the stick and hat and restoring them to the old man.

It is in this scene, too, that we first observe the direction of growth in Jarvis's character. He is moved by the old man's distress and by his humility, and he pulls himself together, resolutely, after the shock of recognition. When his wife's niece returns and says that she dismissed Sibeko's daughter for bad behavior, that she doesn't know where her former servant is, and, what's more, that she doesn't care, Jarvis softens the edge of her rudeness by not translating her "I don't care" into Zulu. The reader is prepared for this softening, in part by what has occurred in this chapter during the encounter with Kumalo, and in part also by the close of the previous chapter, where Jarvis's readings of his son's essays and of passages from Abraham Lincoln opened his mind to change and to the determination to carry on his son's work.

Having formed his resolution, Jarvis goes out from his son's house into a city preoccupied with the discovery of new gold. He is one of those who hear the great bull voice of John Kumalo calling on black workers to demand a fair share of the new wealth. He is disturbed by the revolutionary tone of what he hears, and his son's friend, John Harrison, who is taking him to visit the Claremont African Boys' Club, feels that Jarvis is too old to face this new phenomenon of black activist confrontation.

These events occur in chapter 26, which continues the theme of new gold discoveries—this time, not from the perspective of mine owners and shareholders, but from the point of view of those seeking to unionize black workers. The greater part of this chapter dramatizes the effects of the oratory of John Kumalo on various people. These include Dubula, who organized the bus boycott and the building of Shanty Town, and also Msimangu and Stephen Kumalo.

John Kumalo is here represented as a man gifted with a voice of amazing power, who, if he dared, could stir black men to a frenzy of revolt. All who hear him agree on this. John Kumalo has a good cause, and he presents a good case. After all, he is attacking the same mining interests satirized earlier. But as his associates, Dubula and Tomlinson, know, John Kumalo is not committed to the cause of the downtrodden. He is interested only in himself and in the applause of the crowds. He will not risk losing what he already has—the carpenter's shop, which brings in a good, reliable income, and the adulation of admirers who gather there.

Stephen Kumalo is amazed at his brother's eloquence and his ability to play on the emotions of the crowd. (Paton may intend to suggest some associations with political demagogues, particularly Adolf Hitler.) Msimangu acknowledges John Kumalo's power as an orator, but he also sees him as corrupted by his possessions. Young John Harrison, as already indicated, sees him as representing a new militancy that must be faced and understood by the younger generation; and the police captain, reporting to his superiors, sees him as a dangerous but divided man, lacking the courage to bring his hearers to the point of revolt.

There follow two segments in the voice of a narrator/observer reminiscent of the method of chapter 12. The first of these scenes contemplates the possibility of a strike, and then it sketches a scenario of events that might occur. To white people who realize how dependent they are on black labor, the thought of a miners' strike escalating into a general strike of all black workers is terrifying. Then, in a counterturn, the second segment reports that a strike took place but is now over. There had been some trouble, but it was contained within the mines and did not intrude on the lives of the public. All is now quiet. In the strike's aftermath a few concerned people continue to discuss the case for a black miners' union. At the Johannesburg Anglican Synod a clergyman makes a speech in support of a union; a spokesman for the Chamber of Mines responds that simple miners are not qualified to run a union and would only become the tools of agitators. Others continue their endless talking about social problems without offering to do anything practical.

There is a brief concluding segment from yet another perspective. In it we hear again the prophetic voice that earlier spoke such passages as, for example, "Cry, the beloved country, for the unborn child. . . ." This time it warns against complacency while subterranean forces work beneath the apparently calm surface like the white ants of Africa (a species of termite): "In the deserted harbour there is yet water that laps against the quays. In the dark and silent forest there is a leaf that falls. Behind the polished panelling the white ant eats away the wood. Nothing is ever quiet, except for fools" (190).

F. Charles Rooney sees this passage as "another startling reflection on the inner corruption of South Africa which might seem, at first, extraneous to the story." He adds: "Yet here too we are eventually forced to admit Paton's genius to express his nation's pulse and his people's conscience. Here we see not a lone angry commentator but a compassionate sufferer witnessing the decline of that which he loves. We do not hear the clear voice of the author telling us what to think; these 'asides' always spring from the story: In fact we might wonder at the reticence if they were unsaid, for the very rocks cry out."[3]

The concluding prophetic passage on subterranean forces is all the more powerful in its effect when read with the narrator's earlier comment on the potential of John Kumalo's magnificent voice still in mind—a potential he stops short of using: "What if this voice should say words that it speaks already in private, should rise and not fall again, should rise and rise and rise, and the people rise with it, should madden them with thoughts of rebellion and dominion, with thoughts of power and possession?" (184).

These words may have a more powerful effect on later readers than they had on the first readers in the 1940s. This may derive from the consequences of the passage of time; and on our perception of the march of events in South Africa in approximately half a century since the novel was written. This effect of history, as I remarked in chapter 3, affords present-day readers a perspective on the novel in some ways resembling that of audiences in the Greek tragic theater who knew the outcome of the struggle unfolding on the stage. What to the first readers of *Cry, the Beloved Country* may have seemed merely ominous may appear to more recent readers to foreshadow tragedy. The passage of time may also endow with greater power and foreboding the fear of the hardening of racial attitudes that Msimangu articulates when he says he greatly fears that when the whites are turned to loving, the blacks will have turned to hating.

Chapter 27, the fifth chapter filling the interval between Absalom's trial and sentence, prepares the way for a return to the main story. This chapter is set in the home of Mrs. Lithebe, where Stephen Kumalo is staying with those members of his family he has so far rescued from degradation in the city: his sister Gertrude, her son, and Absalom's pregnant girlfriend. The chapter opens with an encounter in which Mrs. Lithebe rebukes Gertrude for exchanging loose talk and laughter with questionable women and for exerting a bad influence on the young girl.

This interchange between Mrs. Lithebe and Gertrude is but one instance in the novel of a kind of dialogue that Paton handles expertly. Other instances are Kumalo's questioning of Absalom at their prison meeting and, to some degree, his questioning of the girl in Pimville. These exchanges convey convincingly the trapped sullenness of a person who has done wrong but who has no explanation when pressed. Undoubtedly, in the course of his work with delinquent boys at Diepkloof Reformatory, Paton had much experience in such interviews. At one point Gertrude uses an African expression rendered in English as "I hear you." This is an African idiom used simply as a form of respect to someone in authority when the person questioned doesn't have an answer. (Unfortunately, in police interrogations it is sometimes taken as an admission of guilt.)

Gertrude is a divided soul torn between the iniquitous life of the streets and the laudable desire to save her child from that life. She is emotionally unstable and easily swayed by the company she finds herself in. She is moved by the story of the black sister who told of her call to become a nun and renounce the world. She tells Mrs. Lithebe that she, too, wants to become a nun; and she asks the girl to promise to look after her child if she does so. Gertrude represents a psychological type that interested Paton. He explores such a character more fully in his short story "A Divided House" in *Tales from a Troubled Land.* This story is about a delinquent boy, Jacky, who is a habitual thief but who, nevertheless, continues to insist that he wants to be a priest. In his first volume of autobiography, *Towards the Mountain,* Paton has revealed that both characters are based on a boy at Diepkloof Reformatory. In Jacky's case and that of the actual boy at Diepkloof, the thief won out over the priest; and so in Gertrude's case, as we subsequently discover, the prostitute wins out over the nun. When she absconds during the night she leaves behind the new clothes that were the symbol of her renewal.

Gertrude plays no mere incidental part in *Cry, the Beloved Country.* She has an essential, if negative, role in the novel's major theme of rehabilitation and restoration. If the novel were merely sentimental, she would be restored to dignity. But Paton's purpose is to depict the harsh reality that Stephen Kumalo must also come to terms with: though not all can be salvaged, the work of restoration must go on even in the face of such failures. One must assume that a great many delinquent youths were restored to useful lives through the work of Paton and his associates at Diepkloof; but it is in the context of recounting an instance of failure that he tells the story of Jacky.

Stephen Kumalo, too, has his failures. From his perspective, his brother, John, is lost to self-interest; his sister, Gertrude, is lost also; and his son, Absalom, even though Kumalo hopes that through the ministry of Father Vincent he will make his peace with God, is lost to the life his father had anticipated for him. As it turns out, Kumalo is able to bring only a pitiful remnant of family survivors back to Ndotsheni: Gertrude's little son and the girl who is to bear Absalom's child. Edmund Fuller, who writes perceptively of the novel's Christian themes and of the necessity of personal decision in the process of rehabilitation, has this to say of Gertrude: "Gertrude . . . whose degraded state has been the direct cause of Stephen's summons to Johannesburg, is lost. She has gone beyond her personal point of return. The effort of self-examination and rehabilitation is more than she can sustain."[4]

But Gertrude's defection does not occur until after Absalom's sentence, and she is not the only source of interest in this chapter, which serves two essential functions. One of these is to build up tension in anticipation of the judgment on Absalom the following day; and the other is to return us to the main story after the interval of the court's adjournment. It shows Stephen's friends and supporters—Mrs. Lithebe, Msimangu, and the neighbor who hurries in with the newspaper— shocked by the headlines reporting a new murder of a white householder by blacks who had broken in. They fear that the judge may be influenced by these new reports of yet another crime like Absalom's. Wanting to spare Stephen unnecessary suffering, they conspire to hide the newspaper from him and to keep him away from the clergy house where he might see another copy and lose all hope.

chapter 10

Stephen Kumalo:
Towards the Mountain

If we consider the main action of the novel *Cry, the Beloved Country* to be an old father's search for his prodigal son, then the drama of Kumalo's quest seems to reach its climax in Absalom's trial and sentencing. What follows in book 3 may then appear to be, in good measure, anticlimactic. This is what Maxwell Perkins thought at first that some critics might say of the novel. Eventually, he changed his mind. However, since that time, a number of critics who have approached the book solely from a political or sociological viewpoint have been inclined to find the concluding part in some degree "sentimental" as well as anticlimactic. But, from another standpoint, when the book is considered as primarily the story of a Christian priest who is reduced to despair, as Kumalo is in the scene with Father Vincent in book 2, the only logical outcome is either a tragic ending in total despair or its direct opposite: a reaffirmation of faith and hope.

As a priest, Kumalo must either deny or embrace the love of God, which is something beyond his love of Absalom, and which even requires him, in a sense, to endure the biblical trial of Abraham who was directed by God to prepare his only son, Isaac, for sacrifice.

Theologians say that this dimension of love is hard to understand or accept. It is, to use Father Vincent's phrase, "a secret"—which, significantly, is also the phrase on which the novel ends. In the context of literary discussion some appreciation of this level of love may be derived from other works of literature.

In his famous poem, "Among Schoolchildren," the poet W. B. Yeats distinguishes the three kinds of love that, in his words, "passion, piety, and affection know." In this poem Yeats as "a sixty year old smiling public man" from the Education Committee of the Irish Senate is walking through a primary school classroom beside "a kind old nun." Looking at the faces of the young schoolgirls, he is suddenly reminded of the first love of his youth whose name was Maud Gonne and to whom he wrote passionate love poems. He recollects a story she had told him, in an intimate moment, of a sad incident in her own schooldays. Thereupon, he says, she stands before him as a living child, and his heart is driven wild. When, later in the poem, Yeats distinguishes between the three kinds of love: "passion, piety, and affection," *passion* is his word for the love associated with sexual attraction; *affection* is his word for the love of parent for child; and *piety* is his word for the love that draws nuns to consecrate their lives to God.

The life experience of the old clergyman, Stephen Kumalo, in *Cry, the Beloved Country* encompasses love in these three senses. As an Anglican priest he is a married man. Now, on the verge of old age, the mutual love between him and his wife—derived from the love Yeats calls *passion*—is still strong. So is his paternal *affection* for his wayward son that draws him to undertake the arduous quest that is the novel's more conventional theme. But beyond the drive of parental love, the consecrated man, Kumalo, draws strength from the kind of love Yeats ascribes to nuns and for which he employs the term *piety*. It appears that by *piety* in this context, Yeats has in mind the love of God characterized by a sacrifice of self that is sometimes described by the Greek word *agape*. This is the religious love that, in Saint Paul's phrase, encompasses "faith, hope, and charity"—virtues incumbent as a moral obligation on a Christian priest like Kumalo.

Stephen Kumalo: Towards the Mountain

These are the things Father Vincent reminds him of in the "confessional" scene.

If the profession of the protagonist in this novel had been a more conventional one—if he had been, for example, a lawyer, a schoolmaster, or an accountant—we might envision a different development of the plot. With a nonclerical protagonist we might see the plot as comprising a tragic sequence of events: first, the father's quest for his son; second, the murder; third, the intertwining of events involving the victim's father; and finally, the outcome of these. But in *Cry, the Beloved Country* the priesthood of the protagonist invites us to enter a realm beyond tragedy and to witness a resolution on a higher plane. This is the spiritual level at which Kumalo's religious faith is tested to the verge of despair. In his case, despair is not to be seen as merely an intense emotion or deep depression, but, as both Msimangu and Father Vincent at different times remind him, despair is the ultimate sin of a man consecrated to God. Consequently there must be for Kumalo, in liturgical terms, repentance and reconciliation, and also the restoration of love—all of which are themes of book 3 at various levels.

A consideration of the spiritual level of Kumalo's quest provides some justification for Paton's method of developing his central character and of bringing his novel to its conclusion. That this has sometimes been missed by commentators may be understandable. Even so highly qualified a reader as Scribner's editor Max Perkins missed it at first. Much less understandable, however, is the way in which Maxwell Anderson and Kurt Weill, composers of the musical version of the novel, *Lost in the Stars*, overlooked essential aspects of Kumalo's character, including the profound significance of the final stages of his agony on the mountain.

In October 1949, Paton journeyed eagerly to New York for the final rehearsals and Broadway opening of *Lost in the Stars*, but he was both embarrassed and shocked by what he encountered. He attended a rehearsal which he found to be, as he said in the second volume of his autobiography, *Journey Continued*, "an unnerving and at times painful experience." Except for those parts of the musical that reproduced the actual language of the book, he found the stage version unfamiliar. In his view, Todd Duncan, the singer playing the part of Kumalo, "the humble and unsophisticated black priest," was highly sophisticated. So were the lyrics he sang. Paton found it "extremely painful" to hear his humble hero in a role he could never have taken. But what was even more painful to him was the fact that the title song, "Lost in the Stars," belonged, as he said, to "the death-of-God genre, or to put it more accurately, to the desertion-of-God genre."[1]

The theme of Anderson's title song, as Paton said, quoting from the lyrics, is that God had created the earth, "but now he had gone away, 'forgetting the promise that we heard him say'; so 'we are lost out here in the stars'."[2] In light of the discussion of Kumalo's priesthood in the opening section of this chapter, these lines from the lyrics are profoundly unChristian and tantamount to an invitation to despair, and therefore they are an expression of something directly opposed to what Paton intended his character to embody.

Lost in the Stars opened on Broadway to critical acclaim. As Paton remembered it, "People wept and shouted and clapped." The eminent theater critic, Brooks Atkinson, wrote in the *New York Times* that a memorable musical drama had come out of a memorable novel; and another New York critic, Howard Barnes, said that Anderson had "captured the full essence of the original." Paton says in *Journey Continued* that he did his best to join in the rejoicing but his heart was not in it. He also says that he found Anderson's view of the world very different from his own. Anderson, he felt, described himself correctly as an unbeliever: "He was not an atheist, and certainly not a militant one. In fact, if *Lost in the Stars* is to be taken seriously, he believed that there had been a Creator and that he had gone away leaving us lost out here in the stars."[3] As suggested earlier, nothing could have been further from Paton's purpose in *Cry, the Beloved Country*. It is therefore not surprising that he found *Lost in the Stars* less than satisfactory.

Certain aspects of the world of show business that Paton encountered for the first time when *Lost in the Stars* was in production may have added to his sense of displeasure. The song "Lost in the Stars," from which the musical derived its title, was not, in fact, written for a musical version of Paton's novel, nor was it in any way informed by it. Anderson and Weill had written it years before in another context, but it was not then used. They took advantage of the opportunity to use it in their musical of *Cry, the Beloved Country* where Paton rightly felt it didn't belong. To compound the injury, they called the musical by the song's title; and they did this because they and their associates would not call it *Cry, the Beloved Country* unless Sir Alexander Korda of London Films, who was making a film of that title, agreed to pay them a fee on the grounds that their Broadway production would give the film free publicity. Korda refused to pay the fee, so the musical remained *Lost in the Stars*. (Another clause in the contract for the musical decreed that there could be no other stage version of the novel in the United States. That is why there is no significant play derived from this work that is so dramatic in its method.)

During the filming of *Cry, the Beloved Country*, Paton found Alexander Korda much more sympathetic and more understanding of his work than he had found Maxwell Anderson. While Korda, a Hungarian exile who loathed Stalin and Communism, could be very difficult, Paton felt that they had in common a love of freedom and the rule of law and a hatred of authoritarianism. His relationship with Korda, and the fact that he had a part in preparing the script, no doubt enabled him to ensure that the film, unlike the musical, would depict his hero as a humble priest.

In the opening chapters of *Cry, the Beloved Country* we are made aware of Kumalo's failings. His pride, his fear of ridicule, and his sense of self-esteem will not allow him to admit that a man of a parson's standing is ignorant of the world outside the reserve. He pretends to know about train journeys and the big city; but in fact, he lies. Now, at the beginning of book 3, he must return to his own people who know him and his story. He must present himself humbly before them bringing with him the child of his prostitute sister and also the pregnant girl, the wife of his son who has been convicted of murder and sentenced to die.

The people accept him gladly in a service of reconciliation; but there still remains a time of waiting while his son's sentence is appealed to the higher courts. If these appeals fail, there is the day of execution to be endured, in faith or in despair. Meanwhile he must continue to go forward in hope, remembering the friendship and support of Msimangu and the counsel of Father Vincent, who urged him not to try to understand the secret ways of God but to do the practical things that were within reach.

It is at this juncture that interpretations of *Cry, the Beloved Country* face the dual risk of, on the one hand, uncritical applause from those who share Paton's Christian perspective and, on the other hand, of charges of sentimentality from those who do not. But it is precisely at this point, as if to preempt either of these approaches in an extreme form, that Paton appears to raise questions concerning the courses of action open to a practical man as opposed to those that are impractical or utopian. His implicit response contrasts two ways of undertaking the relief of present suffering.

As I have said on this point elsewhere, one way to relieve suffering is to hope for an ideal solution, possibly through the intervention of some agency of state equipped with theoretical, long-range programs. Another way is to accept a measure of responsibility and take practical steps, however small, in the immediate present.[4] Kumalo has heard Father Vincent recommend this method, and he has seen it carried out in Johannesburg by people like Dubula who set up Shanty Town and also the workers at the reformatory and at Ezenzeleni. These "good" characters in the novel act as they do because they are involved in mankind and are in some real sense their brothers' keepers. It is a simple personal assumption of the responsibility of priestly brotherhood by Msimangu that informs Kumalo about his sister's "sickness" and initiates his quest.

Kumalo learns in Johannesburg that he, too, bears a measure of personal responsibility for alleviating suffering: "the great city had opened his eyes to something that had begun and must now be continued" (230). He decides to seek an interview with the chief to discuss practical ways of alleviating the consequences of the drought in Ndotsheni. He next seeks out the schoolmaster who has nothing to offer but theoretical schemes. Paton mocks the schoolmaster's abstract academic jargon about relating the life of the child to the life of the community. The schoolmaster brings Kumalo out in the blazing sun to see the school gardens, but this, too, is an academic exercise. There is no water and everything is dead. Against this background of futility and high-sounding schemes, James Jarvis's simple, practical act of providing milk for the sick children is set with purposeful irony. For it is not only because of the drought that everything is dead but because the schemes and theories themselves are arid. It is only when Jarvis and Kumalo, both grieving for their sons, meet humbly as two human beings, each aware of the other's suffering and therefore of their common humanity, that the drought breaks and the rain comes at last to the valley of Ndotsheni.

In the course of this process of transformation, the small boy who "had a brightness in him" enters as something of a catalyst. He represents a possibility of hope for the future. His father, Arthur Jarvis, the murdered man, had already traveled a long way toward complete freedom from white South African inhibitions and prejudices. The small boy is an imaginative projection or idealized picture of how, in the next generation, the son of such a man might turn out. The characterization of the small boy with his love of words, his eagerness to learn Zulu, and his mingled brightness and seriousness, is an extraordinarily successful little cameo in its own right. The appeal of this cameo may owe much to the fact that Paton, being away from home for months and thinking of his own wife and children—and particularly of his youngest son, Jonathan, who was of an age with the small boy— put some deep personal feelings and longing into the portrait. To the degree that Paton embodied his own ideals in the character of Arthur Jarvis, he also embodied his hopes for his son in the small boy. There is a good measure of reality in this hope. Jonathan was growing up in Diepkloof Reformatory in a nonracial environment unmatched elsewhere in South Africa, on familiar terms with the African teachers and their families, and also with Afrikaans-speaking instructors like the young social worker who helped Kumalo. Such a person would have a shorter road out from the closed world of South African race prejudice than anyone of an earlier generation.

Another character met for the first time in book 3 is the young and enthusiastic black agricultural instructor whose expert knowledge and self-confidence offers a sharp contrast to the old chief and his advisers. This young man carries with him the aura of something new—not only of the renewal of the land but of hope for improving the lot of his people. He is not a utopian idealist. He tells Kumalo bluntly that even if the land is restored, the valley will not provide for all; nor will it keep the people from the big city: "We can restore the valley for those who are here, but when the children grow up, there will be again too many. Some will have to go still" (268). Furthermore, to Kumalo's surprise, the young instructor takes pride in an African national image: "We work for Africa, he said, not for this man or that man. Not for white man or black man, but for Africa." When Kumalo asks why he does not say South Africa, he responds thoughtfully: "We would if we could." And he adds: "We speak as we sing . . . for we sing 'Nkosi Sikelel' iAfrika' " (269). Here, too, in this rural backwater, we find hope embodied in the song that comforted the builders of Shanty Town as they sang it softly in the night. This song, "God Bless Africa," is, at this point, the single common thread uniting the aspirations of the urban and rural poor.

Any account of the young agricultural instructor Napoleon Letsitsi brings up again the question of the generosity of James Jarvis. Having earlier donated one thousand pounds to the Claremont African Boys' Club, Jarvis brings Napoleon Letsitsi to Ndotsheni at his own expense. He contributes the money required for the construction of a dam, and he also donates money to build Kumalo a new church. His white neighbors find such generosity incomprehensible. They feel that Jarvis has lost his senses: "They say he's going queer. From what I've heard, he soon won't have any money left" (243). The nature of Jarvis's generosity has also been inconceivable to those critics who perceive the characterization of Jarvis in book 3 as either unconvincing or sentimental. Even an otherwise favorable critic, Charles J. Rolo, while acclaiming the novel in the

Atlantic Monthly, finds Paton's symbolism in book 3 to be in some degree a failure: "The comfort is unfortunately a trifle pat: milk for the sick child, a new church, a dam for the stricken valley. But if Mr. Paton's symbolism fails him in his final pages, his message loses nothing of its urgency."[5]

However unconvincing Jarvis's generosity may appear, it seems possible that Paton may have had in mind an instance of exceptional generosity from among his own acquaintances; in particular the generosity of his friend, Acting Prime Minister Jan Hofmeyr. In his *Hofmeyr* Paton recounts that Hofmeyr and his mother, who was dependent on him, lived frugally all their lives. They even saved a substantial sum from his Rhodes Scholarship money at Oxford University. Hofmeyr had no private means. According to Paton, he delayed entering politics until he felt he had saved enough from his salary as principal of Witwatersrand University to be financially independent. Later, when he felt his savings were sufficient to provide modestly for himself and his mother in retirement, he established a private trust fund for African education; and he paid eighty percent of his ministerial salary into this fund each year. He did this, Paton says, "out of thanks to God for the mercies of his mother and his honors and his industrious life."[6] After Hofmeyr's death the trust fund was handed over to the Jan Hofmeyr School of Social Work to open up that profession to African men and women. This school, so generously endowed, has continued to flourish in the intervening half-century.

Book 3 of *Cry, the Beloved Country* concludes with Kumalo's journey to the mountain called Emoyeni to spend the night in prayer awaiting the dawn of his son's execution. He had made this penitential journey three times before in his life in moments of grave spiritual crisis. Now in old age he takes the penitential road for the fourth time to keep his painful vigil. On the way his path crosses that of James Jarvis once again. The two fathers, communicating hesitantly across the boundaries of their different worlds, are brought together through the tragedies of their sons and also by the wider tragedy of South Africa.

The theme of the relationships between fathers and sons is not as fully developed in this novel as it is in Paton's second novel, *Too Late the Phalarope*. It flows submerged, as it were, a little below the surface, strengthened by tributary currents from the symbolism of the name *Absalom* and also from general associations with the parable of the prodigal son. As mentioned earlier, it is a theme that appears to have held a special interest for Paton whose relationship with his own father was, at times, very difficult. In his autobiography, *Towards the Mountain,* Paton says that he had a happy childhood except for one thing: "the authoritarian and arbitrary rule of my father, which my mother tempered when she was able."[7] His Scottish-born father was a member of a strict fundamentalist sect. He lived, Paton says, by a narrow morality and insisted on obedience in trivial things. He died tragically. After he had been missing from home for some weeks, his corpse was discovered half-submerged in a mountain stream, stripped of possessions.

Following the encounter with Jarvis, Kumalo continues his journey toward the mountain. This final episode in *Cry, the Beloved Country,* like some of the earlier lyric episodes, has a purposeful symbolic structure derived, in this instance, from the liturgical sequence of the Anglican eucharistic service or the Catholic mass: penitence, thanksgiving, praise, and communion. On the mountain Kumalo first confesses his sins. He recalls those transgressions the reader has already noted in the course of the novel: his lie on the train; his angry lie to his brother, John; his desire to hurt the girl; and, above all, his loss of faith at the worst moments of crisis in Johannesburg.

Kumalo may have little to repent of in the first liturgical stage; but, in the second, he finds much to be thankful for—so much, in fact, that as he enumerates in his mind the long list of things for which he gives thanks he falls asleep. This is something he had never done before on his solitary vigils. When he awakes he prays for all those known to him who are suffering, particularly Absalom awaiting execution. He thinks of his wife and of Msimangu and of the young agricultural instructor; and he thinks also of all the people of Africa, the beloved country. He recalls the hymn, *"Nkosi Sikelel' iAfrika,"* "God

Save Africa," and he wonders why the white rulers fear what people like himself and Msimangu and Napoleon Letsitsi wanted, which was simply "that men should walk upright in the land where they were born, and be free to use the fruits of the earth" (276). Musing on Msimangu's grave and sombre words on love and hate, the old man dozes again.

Awaking with a start the second time, he finds a place among the rocks where he can look to the east and discern the first signs of dawn—the time of his son's execution. His actions at this point recall the eucharistic liturgy at the moment when the bread and wine are placed on the altar and consecrated with words drawn from the New Testament account of Christ's last supper: "On the night he was betrayed, he took the bread and gave thanks and praise. He broke the bread . . . and he gave the cup to his disciples. . . ." As Kumalo takes the food and the tea from the package given him by his wife, he is disturbed at the thought of his son's execution: "He looked out of his clouded eyes at the faint steady lightening in the east. But he calmed himself, and he took out the heavy maze cakes and the tea, and put them upon a stone. And he gave thanks, and broke the cakes and ate them, and drank the tea" (277). As the east brightens with the rising sun, Kumalo rises, uncovers his head, and prays for his son. Throughout his night of tribulation, subconsciously reenacting the sacred rites of his priestly function, he had remained faithful to his calling.

Even though *Cry, the Beloved Country* has tragic qualities that seem to gain intensity with time, its mood is not unremittingly tragic, which is to say that its ending is not despair. The tragedy is relieved by a note of hope—not a faint, sentimental note of hope, akin to whistling past the graveyard in the dark, but a firm one based on the realization that, like Kumalo and Jarvis, all persons have the capacity for good as well as for evil. The brief concluding passage turns aside from Kumalo's private agony to the agony of the beloved country. The dawn has come as always: "But when the dawn will come of our emancipation, from the fear of bondage and the bondage of fear, why, that is a secret" (277).

chapter 11

Some Conclusions

Between the publication of *Cry, the Beloved Country* in 1948 and the death of Alan Paton on 12 April 1988, the social and political fabric of the African continent underwent a great transformation: more than forty former colonial territories emerged as newly independent states. In South Africa, too, where the repressive policies of apartheid had endured for a generation, there was evidence of a new willingness to change. But even in the face of remarkable transformation in the social background, the novel's enduring themes retain their potency, particularly the theme of the acceptance of moral responsibility for beneficent change.

More than once in his speeches and writings, Alan Paton has recalled the inscription on a tablet in an old Yorkshire church that he first heard of from Jan Hofmeyr: "In the year 1652 when through England all things sacred were either profaned or neglected, this church was built by Sir Robert Shirley, Bart. [Baronet], whose special praise it is to have done the best of things in the worst of times and to have hoped them in the most calamitous."[1] With a little modification this "special praise" might supply an apt inscription on memorial tablets to Stephen Kumalo and James Jarvis in the church built through their efforts in Ndotsheni.

Rather than waiting for time or governments to bring about change, each of these characters sets about doing whatever good is within his power; for each has come to recognize how individual fear and indifference infects society with moral paralysis, and each also realizes that the antidote to moral paralysis is individual courage and willingness to go forward in faith. They do not wait for some miraculous healing of this paralysis to be brought about by the direct intervention of God, or through the implementation of some theoretical scheme for a final solution, or through the flowering of some political manifesto. As noted earlier, this theme of the acceptance of personal responsibility for change is also the theme of Paton's two major biographies: *Hofmeyr* and *Apartheid and the Archbishop*. It is also the theme of his three volumes of autobiography: *For You Departed, Towards the Mountain,* and *Journey Continued.*

This theme of the value of individual responsibility may be unpalatable to ideological thinking on both the left and the right of the political spectrum. Consequently both Paton and his work have been subjected from time to time to vehement attack from both extremes. For years, while the South African government mercilessly pursued its policies of apartheid, Paton, as a leader of the nonracial Liberal party, was constantly harassed by members of the security police, who were obtrusively present at meetings, searched his home as well as the party offices, and even, on one occasion, deliberately smashed the windshield of his car. He was arrested more than once, and he also had his passport taken away for ten years.

Later, when extreme opponents of apartheid adopted a policy of violence, he remained committed to nonviolence and constitutional change; and he opposed the strategy of commercial sanctions against South Africa on the grounds that the poor suffered disproportionately through unemployment. This stand exasperated some proponents of the antiapartheid movement on the Left and may have provided some incentive for attacks on his work from that perspective. For example, a review of his posthumous volume, *Journey Continued,* in the *New York Times Book Review* was rather maliciously entitled "Moderate to a Fault?" This review sought to show that Paton's sympathies lay with white rather than black aspirations. It said, disparagingly, that "his heroes were all white men like Hofmeyr and Archbishop Clayton";[2] when, in fact, Paton's heroes included Mahatma Gandhi and leaders of the African National Congress like Professor Z. K. Matthews and Chief Albert Luthuli, the Nobel Peace Prize laureate, whose portrait hung above Paton's writing desk, and at whose funeral in 1967 he delivered an eloquent and defiant eulogy, surpassed as a tribute to Luthuli only by Paton's even more eloquent address at the unveiling of Luthuli's tombstone in 1972. Had the reviewer known these, and had he also read *Apartheid and the Archbishop,* he would have recognized that there is nothing in the rather dutiful biography of Archbishop Clayton to compare with the emotion and eloquence of the tributes to Chief Luthuli.

This review written by William Minter, also refers to Paton's role in the Liberal party, "which from 1953 to 1968 worked within the white electoral system for racial equality."[3] In fact, the membership of the Liberal party, although at first predominantly white, soon became, under Paton's leadership, predominantly black and could no longer work within the white electoral system.

Such petty belittlement in an American journal stands in sharp contrast to the generosity of black South Africans who may have differed with Paton but nevertheless respected his stands. One instance is supplied by Eddie Daniels, a black South African and former member of the Liberal party, who spent fifteen years imprisoned on Robben Island at the same time as Nelson Mandela. In fact, the *New York Times* of 10 February 1990, reporting on a visit by Daniels to Mandela three days before the latter's release from prison, described Daniels as "a friend and former Robben Island cellmate" of Mandela's.[4] Daniels had delivered a memorial address on Alan Paton in St. George's Cathedral, Cape Town, on 21 April 1988. He began as follows: "I feel honoured and humble to have been asked to pay tribute to the memory of this great South African. I can assure you that if Mr. Nelson

Mandela was free he too would be paying tribute to this great South African. In 1974 on Robben Island an illegal commemoration ceremony was held to pay tribute to the memory of Mr. Leo Marquard [cofounder with Paton of the Liberal party]. At this ceremony Mr. Mandela, a man of great integrity, spoke eloquently of the role that the Liberal party had played in the fight against apartheid."[5]

Eddie Daniels was probably right in his surmise that Nelson Mandela would have paid tribute to Alan Paton's fight against apartheid. In 1960 Mandela sought out Paton at a Johannesburg conference to congratulate him on the vigor of his public refutation of the charges made against him by the government when his passport was taken away. "He told me I was a fighter," said Paton, "and this coming from him was a compliment I have never forgotten."[6] Paton, in turn, testified "in mitigation of sentence" on Mandela's behalf at the close of Mandela's trial for treason; and he did this because he feared Mandela and those convicted with him would receive the death sentence that was possible under the law. For this Paton endured sharp attacks on his own character by the prosecuting attorney. Twenty years later, in 1984, Winnie Mandela said in *Part of My Soul Went with Him:* "I remember Alan Paton speaking in mitigation of sentence. He was so sincere, a real political colleague; I'll never forget him for that."[7]

Paton did not live to see the reconciliation he had hoped for replace racial strife in South Africa; but should the spirit of reconciliation prevail, his writings, and in particular his first great novel, will no doubt have contributed to that outcome. In 1989, a year after his death, the newly founded Democratic party campaigned for the votes of the white electorate under the slogan "Vote your hopes, not your fears," which seemed to echo a theme of *Cry, the Beloved Country.* And when this new, untried party surprisingly received one out of every four white votes cast in the election, its leader could confidently make a claim that Paton would have been pleased to hear: "There is a viable number of whites in South Africa perfectly prepared to share citizenship with their black brothers."[8]

Paton's extraordinary work as a penal reformer at Diepkloof was canceled out by the advent of apartheid; and the nonracial Liberal party that he helped to build up was declared illegal in 1968. Yet, even in the worst days, he continued to hope that man's capacity for good would prevail. In the course of his Hoernlé Memorial Lecture, titled "Federation or Desolation," delivered before the South African Institute of Race Relations in 1985, he remarked: "In such times as these it is easy to lose hope. Nadezhda Mandelstam, whose husband, the poet Osip Mandelstam, died in 1938 in a 'transit camp' at Vladivostok, wrote a book about their life of unspeakable suffering under Stalin. This book she called *Hope Against Hope*. After his death she wrote a second book, and wished it to be called in English *Hope Abandoned*. In South Africa we are still writing the first book. We trust that we shall never have to write the second."[9]

Paton had entered on the political scene in South Africa in the 1950s because he was convinced that the mounting injustices of apartheid required him to do what he could to oppose it and not because he had a love of politics. He wrote and spoke eloquently and, at times, passionately, on behalf of racial justice and also on behalf of the program of the Liberal party that opposed all forms of totalitarianism including fascism and communism.

That he was a reluctant politician, whose first love was language and the power of words, is poignantly manifest in the last and unfinished piece of writing of his life. He had been approached by the magazine *Time* for an essay on the topic "South Africa Today"; but at eighty-five and already burdened by his last illness, what he wrote was not an essay on current affairs but a farewell to language: a retrospective view of his love of poetry and the spoken word—a love that informed his masterpiece, *Cry, the Beloved Country*.

He starts his essay with a comment on the fact that he is eighty-five and no longer surefooted. He turns aside with a note of surprise at not finding the word *surefootedness* in the *Shorter Oxford Dictionary*, but he is relieved to find it in *Webster's*. (True lovers of words like Paton are haunters of dictionaries: they revere language as a gift from generations past, not as a private affair of their own invention.) Then he confesses: "My creative and literary imagination will never again rise to any great height. I shall never again write words like these"[10]; and he quotes a passage from the opening of *Cry, the Beloved Country* beginning: "The great red hills stand desolate, and the earth has torn away like flesh. . . ."; and he also quotes some lines from his poem, "A Small Boy Who Died at Diepkloof Reformatory."

These lines on death lead him into the topic of great memorial verse. He expresses gratitude for his continuing love of the word and for his ability to recapture the emotion he first felt on reading certain pieces. In illustration he quotes from Whitman's memorial to Lincoln, "When Lilacs Last in the Dooryard Bloom'd" which he calls "one of the most memorable tributes paid by any human being to another." He says he would like to have written William Blake's poem "The Tyger," Francis Thompson's "The Hound of Heaven," or W. B. Yeats's "The Fiddler of Dooney."

In his last years, Paton developed a great admiration for Yeats. He once wrote to ask me about recordings of Yeats reading his own work, and I supplied him with what was available. These were undoubtedly the source of his remarks on Yeats reading his own poems in *Journey Continued*. He grew particularly fond of "The Fiddler of Dooney," and he included it in his address honoring South Africa's first black novelist, "The Sol Plaatje Memorial for 1987," at the University of Bophuthatswana. He said in commentary:

> Yeats must have felt very pleased when he had written "The Fiddler of Dooney"; and he probably felt grateful too, that he had been given the gift of making such music. But that is not the point I wish to make. The point I want to make is that such a poem simply could not be written in South Africa today. It has no pain it it, it has no bitterness in it, it has no racial undertones or overtones, though Yeats could write poetry with all these characteristics. "The Fiddler of Dooney" is a song, and a merry song too, but as James Matthews wrote: "I cannot join in their merriment." No one can write a merry song in South Africa today.[11]

At about the time Paton gave that lecture I sent him a draft of the script of my play on Yeats, *I Am of Ireland*, then in rehearsal at the

Abbey Theatre in Dublin. He wrote back in his inimitable pose of testiness to complain that he could not understand why such a work on Yeats should omit "The Fiddler of Dooney." (He did not live to know that the poem was subsequently restored to the script, partly in tribute to his memory.)

Paton's unfinished essay for *Time* turns, in its latter part, to the topic of great speakers of the English language. He begins with the theologian Reinhold Niebuhr, recalling that he first heard Niebuhr speak at Friends' House, London, in July 1946: "One of his themes was the potential goodness of individual man, and the potential wickedness of political man. An individual man could become a saint, but collective man was a tough proposition."[12] It seems likely that, a month or so later, this theme found its way into *Cry, the Beloved Country* in the two major characterizations: Stephen Kumalo and James Jarvis.

Paton then turns to a recollection of the masters of the spoken word in South Africa, "General Smuts and his lieutenant J. H. Hofmeyr," recalling how the latter quoted the inscription on the tablet to the memory of Sir Robert Shirley in a great speech in 1939 when the threat of Hitler and a new world war hung over the world. At the point where his last manuscript breaks off, Paton had turned to his fourth master of the spoken word: "The fourth and greatest speaker of my time was Winston Churchill, in the days of the Second World War. He was possibly the greatest speaker of English in the history of the language."[13]

Paton's son, Jonathan, added in a note: "He told me he intended adding some comments made by Churchill at the end of his life, and then, ironically, he would add something about the end of his own life." But he may have already written this; for his eloquent tribute to the power of the spoken word brings a fitting close to the literary career of the author of *Cry, the Beloved Country*, a book as memorable for the poetic appeal of its language as for its serious theme of human responsibility.

Notes and References

Chapter 1

1. Alan Paton, *Cry, the Beloved Country,* with an introduction by Edward Callan (New York: Collier Books, Macmillan Co., 1987), 172; hereafter cited in the text.

2. This English translation of Anna Steenkamp's letter is a staple of South African history texts. It is quoted here from Alan Paton, *Hope for South Africa* (London: Pall Mall, 1956), 27. For details of original, see G. S. Preller, *Voortrekkermense* (Kaapstad, 1918–22), II: 30.

Chapter 2

1. Orville Prescott, *In My Opinion: An Inquiry into the Contemporary Novel* (New York: Bobbs-Merrill, 1952), 240.

2. Nadine Gordimer, "English-Language Literature and Politics in South Africa," in *Aspects of South African Literature,* ed. Christopher Heywood (London: Heinemann, 1976), 108.

3. Edmund Fuller, *Books with Men behind Them* (New York: Random House, 1962), 101.

4. Horton Davies, *A Mirror for the Ministry in Modern Novels* (New York: Oxford University Press, 1959), 135.

5. F. Charles Rooney, "The 'Message' of Alan Paton," *Catholic World* 194 (1961): 94.

6. Alan Paton, *Towards the Mountain* (New York: Scribner, 1980), 300.

7. Edward Callan, introduction to *Cry, the Beloved Country,* by Alan Paton (New York: Collier Books, Macmillan Co., 1987), xxiii.

Chapter 3

1. Paton, *Towards the Mountain*, 292.

2. A. Scott Berg, *Max Perkins: Editor of Genius* (New York: Pocket Books, 1978), 556.

3. Berg, 556.

4. Berg, 558.

5. Berg, 559.

6. Berg, 559.

7. Orville Prescott, review of *Cry, the Beloved Country*, *New York Times*, 2 February 1948, 17.

8. *Yale Review* 37 (Spring 1948): 573.

9. Richard Sullivan, review of *Cry, the Beloved Country*, *New York Times Book Review*, 1 February 1948, 6.

10. Margaret Carson Hubbard, review of *Cry, the Beloved Country*, *New York Herald Tribune Weekly Book Review*, 1 February 1948, 4.

11. Sullivan, 6.

12. Lewis Gannet, review of *Cry, the Beloved Country*, *New York Herald Tribune*, 2 February 1948; quoted in Paton, *Towards the Mountain*, 299.

13. Lewis Gannet, introduction to *Cry, the Beloved Country*, by Alan Paton (New York: Scribner Library, 1959), xi–xxix.

14. James Stern, review of *Cry, the Beloved Country*, *New Republic*, 22 March 1948, 26.

15. Charles J. Rolo, review of *Cry, the Beloved Country*, *Atlantic Monthly* 181 (1948): 112.

16. A. W. Foulke, review of *Cry, the Beloved Country*, *Commonweal*, 27 February 1948, 449.

17. Adrienne Koch, review of *Cry, the Beloved Country*, *Saturday Review*, 14 February 1948, 14.

18. Edith James, review of *Cry, the Beloved Country*, *San Francisco Chronicle*, 15 February 1948, 12.

19. *Times Literary Supplement*, 23 October 1948, 593. Reviewed under the common title, "Human Motives," with two other novels: *The Air That Kills* by Francis King and *Tobias Brandywine* by Dan Wickenden.

20. Horton Davies, "Alan Paton: Literary Artist and Anglican," *Hibbert Journal* 50 (1952): 263.

21. Paton, *Towards the Mountain*, 10.

22. Paton, *Towards the Mountain*, 272.

23. *Time*, 4 May 1987, 35.

24. Dennis Brutus, "Protest against Apartheid," in *Protest and Conflict*

in African Literature, ed. Cosmo Pieterse and Donald Munro (New York: Africana Publishing Co., 1969), 95–96.

25. Martin Tucker, *Africa in Modern Literature* (New York: Ungar, 1967), 225.

26. Sheridan Baker, "Paton's Beloved Country and the Morality of Geography," *College English,* 19 (1957): 56; reprinted in *Paton's "Cry, the Beloved Country": The Novel, the Critics, the Setting,* ed. Sheridan Baker (New York: Scribner, 1968), 144–48.

27. Harry A. Gailey, "Sheridan Baker's 'Paton's Beloved Country,' " *College English,* 20 (1958): 143; reprinted in *Paton's Cry,* ed. Baker, 149–50.

Chapter 4

1. Alan Paton, *For You Departed* (New York: Scribner, 1969), 110.

2. "Remarks by Mr. Alan Paton," in *Minutes of a Conference on Urban Juvenile Native Delinquency Held in Johannesburg,* October 1938, 10–11. (From the files of the South African Institute of Race Relations.)

3. Paton, *Towards the Mountain,* 191.

4. Alan Paton, *Hofmeyr* (Cape Town: Oxford University Press, 1964), 293.

5. *Forum,* 26 September 1938; quoted in Paton, *Hofmeyr,* 294–95.

6. Alan Paton, "The Real Way to Cure Crime," *Forum,* 29 January 1944, 24.

7. Alan Paton, "Who Is Really to Blame for the Crime Wave in South Africa?" *Forum,* 15 December 1945, 7–8; source of all quotations in this paragraph.

8. Paton, "Who Is . . . to Blame," 7–8.

9. Alan Paton, *Apartheid and the Archbishop* (New York: Scribner, 1973), 117.

10. Alan Paton, "A Deep Experience," *Contrast* (December 1961): 20–24; reprinted in *The Long View,* by Alan Paton, ed. Edward Callan (New York: Praeger, 1968), 58–59.

11. Paton, *For You Departed,* 88.

Chapter 5

1. Hubbard, 4.

2. J. M. Coetzee, *White Writing: On the Culture of Letters in South Africa* (New Haven: Yale University Press, 1988), 117.

3. Coetzee, 128.

4. Coetzee, 126.

5. Coetzee, 127–28.

6. Coetzee, 129.

7. Coetzee, 129.

8. J. M. Synge, preface to *The Playboy of the Western World* (Dublin: Maunsel, 1907), vii.

9. Alan Paton, interview by John K. Hutchens, *New York Herald Tribune Book Review,* 6 November 1949, 2.

10. W. B. Yeats, *Essays and Introductions* (New York: Macmillan, 1961), 508.

11. Paton, *Towards the Mountain,* 272.

12. Alan Paton, "I Have Approached," *Contrast* 1, no. 4 (December 1961): 17; reprinted in Paton, *The Long View,* 43–44.

13. *New York Times,* 7 April 1987, 15.

14. R. L. Stevenson, "To V. S. Crockett," as quoted in Paton, *Towards the Mountain,* 5.

15. Alan Paton, "The Challenge of Fear," in *What I Have Learned* (New York: Simon and Schuster, 1968), 253.

16. Yeats, 551.

17. Paton, *Towards the Mountain,* 269.

18. John Gross, "Books of the Times," review of *Enigma: The Life of Knut Hamsun,* by Robert Ferguson, *New York Times,* 19 May 1987, 17.

Chapter 6

1. Rooney, 14.

Chapter 7

1. Edward Callan, *Alan Paton,* rev. ed. (Boston: Twayne Publishers, 1982), 8.

Chapter 8

1. Davies, 132.

2. Although Jarvis reads them, these passages from Lincoln are not quoted in the novel.

3. Walt Whitman, "When Lilacs Last in the Dooryard Bloom'd," lines 1–3, as quoted in Paton, *For You Departed,* 59.

4. Alan Paton, "A Literary Remembrance," *Time,* 25 April 1988, 105.

5. Paton, *Towards the Mountain,* 277.

Notes and References

Chapter 9

1. Rooney, 95.
2. Fuller, 96–97.
3. Rooney, 95.
4. Fuller, 99.

Chapter 10

1. Alan Paton, *Journey Continued* (New York: Scribner, 1988), 20.
2. Paton, *Journey*, 20.
3. Paton, *Journey*, 24.
4. Callan, *Alan Paton*, 40.
5. Rolo, 113.
6. Paton, *Hofmeyr*, 417.
7. Paton, *Towards the Mountain*, 27.

Chapter 11

1. Alan Paton, *Federation or Desolation* (Johannesburg: SAIRR, 1985), 12.

2. William Minter, *New York Times Book Review*, 20 November 1988, 36.

3. Minter, 36.

4. "Mandela Meets with Antiapartheid Coalition," *New York Times*, 10 February 1990, 5.

5. Eddie Daniels, "Salute to the Memory," *Reality* 20 (July 1988): 6.

6. Paton, *Journey Continued*, 215.

7. Winnie Mandela, *Part of My Soul Went with Him* (New York: W. W. Norton, 1985), 81.

8. *New York Times*, 8 September 1989, 4.

9. Paton, *Federation or Desolation*, 2.

10. Alan Paton, "A Literary Remembrance," *Time*, 25 April 1988, 105

11. Alan Paton, "The Sol Plaatje Memorial Lecture for 1987," *Reality* 19 (November 1987): 9.

12. Paton, "A Literary Remembrance," 106.

13. Paton, "A Literary Remembrance," 106.

Selected Bibliography

Primary Sources

1. Editions of *Cry, The Beloved Country*

Cry, the Beloved Country. With an introduction by Edward Callan, foreword by Charles Scribner, Jr., and note on the 1987 edition by Alan Paton. New York: Collier Books, Macmillan Co., 1987.

Cry, the Beloved Country. New York: Charles Scribner's Sons, 1948. Dedication: "To Aubrey and Marigold Burns of Fairfax, California." Chapters numbered continuously throughout.

Cry, the Beloved Country: A Story of Comfort in Desolation. London: Jonathan Cape, 1948. Dedication: "To my Wife and to my friend of many years Jan Hendrick Hofmeyr." Chapters numbered within books 1, 2, and 3.

2. Other Novels

Ah, but Your Land Is Beautiful. New York: Charles Scribner's Sons, 1981. Set against the background of the Liberal party period, 1953–68.

Too Late the Phalarope. Cape Town: Cannon (for Jonathan Cape, London), 1953; New York: Charles Scribner's Sons, 1953.

3. Short Stories

Debbie Go Home. London: Cape, 1961. Also published as *Tales from a Troubled Land*.

Tales from a Troubled Land. New York: Charles Scribner's Sons, 1961.

Selected Bibliography

4. Plays

Lost in the Stars (with Maxwell Anderson). New York: Sloane Associates, 1950.

Nkhumbane. Libretto for a musical by Todd Matshikiza, performed at Durban City Hall, 1960. N. p.

Sponono (with Krishna Shah). New York: Charles Scribner's Sons, 1965.

5. Biography

Apartheid and the Archbishop: The Life and Times of Geoffrey Clayton. New York: Charles Scribner's Sons, 1973.

Hofmeyr. Cape Town: Oxford University Press, 1964. Published in abridged form as *South African Tragedy.*

South African Tragedy: The Life and Times of Jan Hofmeyr. Abridged by Dudley C. Lunt. New York: Charles Scribner's Sons, 1965.

6. Autobiography

For You Departed. New York: Charles Scribner's Sons, 1969. Published in London as *Kontakion for You Departed.*

Towards the Mountain. New York: Charles Scribner's Sons, 1980; London: Jonathan Cape, 1981.

Journey Continued. New York: Charles Scribner's Sons, 1988.

7. Essays

"A Literary Remembrance." *Time,* 25 April 1988, 105–6.

"Challenge of Fear." In *What I Have Learned: Essays from the Saturday Review,* 250–60. New York: Simon and Schuster, 1968.

Federation or Desolation. Johannesburg: South African Institute of Race Relations, 1985. Lecture supporting a federal union in South Africa.

"Sol Plaatje Memorial Lecture for 1987." *Reality* 19 (November 1987): 7–11.

"Unveiling of the Albert Lutili Tombstone." *Reality* 4 (September 1972): 5–6.

8. Collected Writings

Knocking on the Door: Shorter Writings of Alan Paton. Edited by Colin Gardner. New York: Charles Scribner's Sons, 1975.

The Long View. Edited by Edward Callan. New York: Praeger, 1968; London: Pall Mall, 1968. A selection of Paton's "Long View" essays from *Contact,* Freedom Award speech, and "A Deep Experience."

Secondary Sources

1. Bibliographies

Bentel, Lea. *Alan Paton: A Bibliography.* Johannesburg: University of the Witwatersrand Department of Bibliography, Librarianship, and Typography, 1969.

Callan, Edward. "Selected Bibliography." In *Alan Paton.* New York: Twayne Publishers, 1968. Contains "juvenilia" and other material not in Bentel.

Callan, Edward, ed., and Rolf Italiaander, comp. *Alan Paton: Hamburger Bibliographien, Band 11.* Hamburg: Hans Christians Varlag, 1970. In German; the most complete listing to date.

2. Books and Parts of Books

Baker, Sheridan. *Paton's "Cry, the Beloved Country": The Novel, the Critics, the Setting.* New York: Charles Scribner's Sons, 1968. A Scribner Research Anthology. Contains selected criticism.

Callan, Edward. *Alan Paton,* rev. ed. Boston: Twayne Publishers, 1982. Survey of Paton's writings to date.

Coetzee, J. M. *White Writing: On the Culture of Letters in South Africa.* New Haven and London: Yale University Press, 1988. Treats Paton's use of Zulu.

Davies, Horton. *A Mirror for the Ministry in Modern Novels.* New York: Oxford University Press, 1959. Gives an analysis of *Cry, the Beloved Country.*

Fuller, Edmund. *Books with Men behind Them.* New York: Random House, 1962. Evaluates Paton's novels.

Prescott, Orville. *In My Opinion.* New York: Bobbs-Merrill, 1952. Evaluates *Cry, the Beloved Country.*

Tucker, Martin. *Africa in Modern Literature.* New York: Unger, 1967. Contains commentary on the novels.

3. Articles

Daniels, Eddie. "Salute to the Memory." *Reality* 20 (July 1988): 6.

Gardner, Colin. "Paton's Literary Achievement." *Reality* 20 (July 1988): 8–11.

Rooney, Charles. "The 'Message' of Alan Paton." *Catholic World* 194 (November 1961): 92–98.

Index

Abrahams, Peter, 23
African National Congress, 112
Anderson, Maxwell, 101–2
Anglo-Boer War, 3, 21, 57, 79
Apartheid, 60, 70, 85–86, 110, 113
Atkinson, Brooks, 102
Auden, W. H., 24, 50

Baker, Sheridan, 23–24
Barnes, Howard, 102
Berg, A. Scott: *Max Perkins*, 14–16
Bible, The (Biblical language), 16, 38–39, 42–44
Blake, William, 115
Botha, General Louis, 8
Brutus, Dennis, 22–23
Broadway (New York Theatre Productions), 101–2
Bunyan: *Pilgrim's Progress*, 24
Burns, Aubrey, 14–16
Burns, Marigold, 14–15
Burt, Cyril: *The Young Delinquent*, 46

Callan, Edward, 13, 23, 115–16
Cape of Good Hope (Cape Province), 3, 5–7, 82
Christians and Jews, Society of, 12, 14
Church and the Nation, The (Anglican Synod report), 35
Churchill, Winston, 116
Clayton, Bishop Geoffrey, 35, 112
Coetzee, J. M., 11; *White Writing*, 40–42
Coleridge, S. T., 92

Da Gama, Vasco, 3
Daniels, Eddie, 112–13
Dante: *Divine Comedy*, 24, 29, 36
Davies, Horton: *A Mirror for Ministry*, 12, 23, 75, 81
Dickens, Charles, 50–51
Diepkloof Reformatory, 8, 20, 29–31, 36, 46, 54–55, 64–65, 96–97, 105, 113
Dutch East India Company, 5, 82

Eliot, T. S.: *The Waste Land*, 69

Fitzgerald, F. Scott, 15
Forum, The, 31–34, 70
Foulke, A. W., 19
Freud, Sigmund, 46
Fugard, Athol, 11
Fuller, Edmund, 11–12, 23, 90

Gailey, Harry A., 23
Ghandi, Mahatma, 65
Gannet, Lewis, 18–19
Gordimer, Nadine, 10–11, 23

Hamsun, Knut: *Growth of the Soil*, 52–53
Hemingway, Ernest, 15, 50
Hersey, John: *The Wall*, 10
Herzog, General J. B. M., 4
Hoernlé, Alfred, 41, 114
Hofmeyr, Jan H., 8, 31–32, 88, 107, 110, 112, 116
Housman, A. E., 51

Index

South Africa, Union of, 3–4; Republic of, 5
Steenkamp, Anna, 6
Steinbeck, John: *The Grapes of Wrath,* 50, 51, 58
Stern, James, 19
Stevenson, R. L., 45
Sullivan, Richard, 17–18
Synge, J. M., 22, 42

Taylor, Peter, 44
Thompson, Francis, 115
Time, 21, 84, 114–16
Times, The (London), 54; Special Book Award, 20
Transvaal, 3, 6–7
Trondheim, Norway, 30, 52–54

Tucker, Martin: *Africa in Modern Literature,* 23

Van der Stel, Simon, 82
Voortrekkers, 4–5, 57

Walpole, Hugh, 51
Weill, Kurt, 101
Whitman, Walt, 84, 115
Wolfe, Thomas, 15
Wordsworth, William, 51

Yeats, W. B., 22, 42, 48–49, 72, 100, 115

Zulu language, 18, 35–42, 52, 75, 93

The Author

Edward Callan is at present Distinguished University Professor, Emeritus, at Western Michigan University, where he received the Distinguished Faculty Scholar Award in 1980. He has been a member of St. Antony's College, Oxford University, and Visiting Professor of English at the University of Michigan. He has a B.A. degree from the University of the Witwatersrand, Johannesburg, an M.A. from Fordham University, New York, and a doctorate degree in literature and philosophy from the University of South Africa, Pretoria. In 1983 he received the Distinguished Faculty Award from the Michigan Association of Governing Boards.

Dr. Callan has written extensively on Alan Paton, whom he has known for many years. He compiled and edited Paton's political writings in *The Long View* (1967), and he provided the introduction to the 1987 Collier Books edition of *Cry, the Beloved Country*. His Twayne's World Authors Series volume, *Alan Paton* (1968), was listed by *Choice: Books for College Libraries* among the "Outstanding Academic Books of 1969"; it was updated in 1982.

Dr. Callan's other works include *Auden* (Oxford University Press, 1983) and *Yeats on Yeats* (Dublin: Dolmen Press, 1981). His play on the poet W. B. Yeats, *I Am of Ireland,* was produced by the Abbey Theatre, Dublin (the Irish national theatre company) for several revivals during 1988–90, and it has toured to London, Rome, Belfast, and the United States.

Dr. Callan was born in Ireland and educated there as well as in England, South Africa, and the United States. He served with a South African division in North Africa and Italy in World War II. His writings on South Africa include the monograph, *Albert John Luthuli and the South African Race Conflict* (Western Michigan University Press, 1962 and 1965).